THE TULIP TREE

The light was going but it was still not too dark to find her way and she flung a shawl over her thin black dress and hurried down to the bowling green once more. She was returning with the doll in her hand when Oliver stopped her at the wicket gate. He did not move as she approached and with her heart sinking she hoped that he was not going to be tiresome again.

'I followed you because I can never see you alone,' he said, his easy smile sure of her forgiveness.

'That is scarcely surprising,' she said stiffly. 'I am employed here as your sister's governess, Lord Fetherstone, not as yours!'

'I wish you would not be so sharp with me. A number of my friends are coming tomorrow and an aunt and cousins to entertain them, and I shall not have a chance of speaking to you while they are here. I meant no harm the other night: it was all a piece of fun, and I thought you would take it that way, I give you my word.'

'It was of no consequence.' She waited for him to move from the gate, gathering her shawl closely about her because the air was cold outside the sheltered bowling green. 'I will say goodnight, my lord.'

The Tulip Tree

Mary Ann Gibbs

CORONET BOOKS
Hodder and Stoughton

Copyright © Mary Ann Gibbs 1979

First published in Great Britain 1979 by
Hurst & Blackett Ltd

Coronet edition 1982

British Library C.I.P.

Gibbs, Mary Ann
The tulip tree. — (Coronet books)
I. Title
823.914 (F) PR6057.I234

ISBN 0 340 267933

Printed and bound in Great Britain for
Hodder and Stoughton Paperbacks, a
division of Hodder and Stoughton Ltd.,
Mill Road, Dunton Green, Sevenoaks,
Kent (Editorial Office: 47 Bedford
Square, London, WC1 3DP) by
©ollins, Glasgow.

I

On the day in the autumn of 1844 when their lawyer,
Mr Cruikshank, told Mrs Lakesby and her daughter
in his dry precise way that their cousin, Eustace
Lakesby, would like to move into Lakesby Manor in six
months' time, Allegra had assured her mother and her
Aunt Bell, who had lived with them since her niece
was born, that there was nothing she would like better
than the house that the lawyer had found for them in
Well Walk in Paragay.

Paragay was a charming little town a few miles away
from Lakesby. It was situated in a valley, with an extensive common broken by outcroppings of rock, and
thickets of hawthorn, sloe bushes and brambles, rising
up behind the town to the top of a hill, where a wooded
lane joined the turnpike and open country beyond.

Well Walk backed on to the common, and an old
friend of Mrs Lakesby's, Mrs Willoughby, had a house
there, which was felt to be a recommendation. Otherwise it was a small paved street, with terraces of select
small houses on either side, and at one end the well
from which it took its name. The well was fenced in
with ornamental iron railings, the brownish water that
bubbled up from the spring beneath having such an
unpleasant taste that visitors still regaled themselves
with it, believing that it must have beneficial qualities,
although the time when the town had been a spa was
long past.

From beside the well steps led down to the Upper
Colonnade, a shallow crescent of shops set in a sheltered
promenade, while the entrance to Well Walk was from

Market Street, which in turn led into Market Square. Here country people came on a Friday to sell butter and eggs and live chickens and ducks, and country produce of all kinds, the cattle market being next to the railway station at the bottom of the town.

The Upper Colonnade was separated from a Lower Colonnade by a stretch of grass and tall trees, benches being placed there for the elderly and much used by nursemaids with young children. The Lower Colonnade was not considered so genteel: it is true that there was the church of St Stephen the Martyr at the Market Street end, but the churchyard adjoined an extensive livery stables, owned by the Coach and Horses Inn, a lodging much favoured by the coachmen and servants of visitors to the town. On the other side of the Coach and Horses were the Paragay Assembly Rooms, a focus of social activity, the monthly balls there being patronized occasionally by some of the leading families in the county, if the weather made the roads to Paragay possible.

The Market Square was surrounded by offices – in one of which Mr Cruikshank conducted his business – a private bank, Horrock's, a cordwainer, a grocer or two, a butcher, a baker and a pastrycook, and shops selling ironware and farming necessities.

Mrs Lakesby was too much of an invalid to enjoy late nights, but when her daughter Allegra was seventeen she had attended some of the balls at the Assembly Rooms under the wing of their old friend, Lady Alicia Tremayne, and her daughters, Allegra being the same age as the youngest girl, Charlotte. She had also enjoyed driving in from Lakesby with her Aunt Bell on shopping expeditions, visiting the select shops in the Upper Colonnade, where jewellery and the finest lace and millinery could be purchased, and where it was possible to buy the best-quality French gloves, and silk

6

stockings. Part of the charm of those visits had been the noise and bustle of the market on a Tuesday or a Friday, when she could persuade her aunt to stand for a moment to listen with amusement to the patter of the cheapjacks.

In those halcyon days life at Lakesby had stretched out before her as one that had no end. She knew that as her father had no son the house and estates were entailed to a distant cousin, Eustace Lakesby, but the thought of Henry Lakesby's death was a prospect as remote as the Continent of Europe. She had never allowed herself to dwell on it for a moment, her father being still in his mid-forties and to her mind almost immortal. His death therefore, of a sudden seizure, six months after her eighteenth birthday, was a shock doubled by the realization that she and her mother now had no home.

Eustace Lakesby was not an unfeeling man, but he had a clear head for business, and on discovering that the property he had inherited was so heavily encumbered with debt that it would be several years before he could hope to receive any benefit from its rents, he warned Mrs Henry that he would be forced to sell his London house and move to the Manor. He advised her to consult her lawyer about moving to Paragay, where she had friends, where the shops were known to her and the tradespeople obliging, and where she could obtain a modest and inexpensive dwelling. The Dower House in Lakesby village to which she could have moved he proposed to give to his son Robert, as to live there would be far beyond her means.

Number 14 in Well Walk was inspected by the widow and her daughter and her sister-in-law, Miss Bell Lakesby, and declared to be sufficient for their needs, and in less than six months after Henry Lakesby's funeral the move was completed. Allegra welcomed the

7

speed with which it was done: if she had to be cut off from her beloved Lakesby let the knife be sharp and the severance complete.

At first she had been determined to like her new home, although when the furniture was all moved in – and they had been careful to select only small items from the Manor – it was extraordinary how a house that had looked roomy, if not actually spacious, became suddenly overcrowded and cramped.

It was odd, too, to see houses across the street from her bedroom window instead of spreading lawns, but it was not until the last cupboard had been made, the last bookshelf fitted, and the chintz curtains hung at her window to hide the shutters that guarded her privacy at night, that a remark from the little maid Lucy who had hung the curtains brought home to her what had happened.

'There!' she said with satisfaction, as she removed the kitchen chair on which she had been standing. 'That looks more like 'ome, don't it, Miss Allegra?'

Allegra smiled but made no answer, and after Lucy had gone she sat down on her bed and stared at the window and its pretty curtains and the houses opposite and thought, 'More like home? But home is where the heart is and mine is still at Lakesby.'

She did her best to hide her growing disillusion for Paragay and their little house. Indeed Number 14 Well Walk would have been regarded by some as a very pleasant small house. It was set in the middle of a quiet street, its grey-slated roof in excellent repair, and its red-brick walls dating back to the reign of Queen Anne, when the spa had been in its hey-day. As for accommodation, it possessed two attics, the larger of which was occupied by Paisley, Mrs Lakesby's personal maid, and the smaller by Lucy, to whose services with Paisley's they were now reduced. Below the attics were three bedrooms and two dressing-rooms, and on the ground floor a parlour, a dining-parlour, and a little breakfast-room that overlooked a walled garden backing on to the common.

But with the exception of Dr Sibley and his wife and noisy family of small boys on the corner, the other residents of Well Walk were all getting on in years. Lady Grant, who lived opposite Number 14 with a cross-grained companion, was at least fifty, while Major Latimer at Number 12 lived alone there with a man-servant and a cook and was nearer sixty. Then there were the two Miss Dalrymples, middle-aged ladies who snubbed Bell if they saw her out with a basket on her arm, having a housekeeper to shop for them, and Mrs Lakesby's friend, Mrs Willoughby at Number 20, next to the well, and she appeared to have only one topic of conversation, her grandson who was a midshipman in the Navy.

Letting her thoughts flit from one to another of her new acquaintances in Paragay it seemed to Allegra that the only girls near her age were the Rector's daughters. They were friendly but full of good works, and she was unable to share their enthusiasm for bazaars, and teaching in the Sunday school, and making garments for the poor, while flirting with their papa's curates. She never called at the Rectory without finding the girls gathered round the dining-table, cutting out red flannel, or just about to set out on some errand of mercy, or else discussing the newest curate with blushes and laughter.

In the meantime Eustace and his family did their best to show their cousins every kindness and to welcome them to Lakesby when they could be persuaded to come. Mrs Henry was always pleased to see the Manor again, if only to assure herself that the family portraits were in their usual places and that the violet beds had not been dug up. Eustace was a stern man but

9

not ungenerous: he paid the rent of Number 14 and the window tax, while servants would arrive twice a week from Lakesby with fruit and vegetables and fresh eggs, besides strawberries in the summer and peaches from the hot-houses, the bearers of such luxuries being rewarded in the kitchen by Paisley with gossip and glasses of small beer.

Eustace's only son Robert was a younger and more energetic version of his father. He was married and soon settled down with his wife and family of three small children in the Dower House: he had an independent income of one thousand a year left him by his godfather, while his wife Elaine had brought a small fortune with her. She was a nice, gentle girl, and from the first had shown her sympathy for Allegra in having been turned out of her old home. When she came into Paragay she would never fail to call at Number 14 to see how they all did, and to bring flowers from the Dower House.

All this was accepted by Mrs Henry Lakesby and Bell with gratitude and pleasure, while Allegra did her best to hide her secret resentment. In that first spring and summer after they left Lakesby she found it unbearable that comparative strangers should be free to pick the Lakesby flowers and dispose of the fruit and vegetables there as they would. She found herself even growing angry with Bell when, with her usual cheerfulness and good humour, she expressed the warm thanks of them all.

Bell found great pleasure in tending the little garden in Well Walk, growing old-fashioned flowers like pinks and sweet peas and larkspur and hollyhocks, mixed with solid cabbage roses and Dutch honeysuckle. When she felt in the mood Allegra would sow a few flower seeds under the breakfast-room window, but try as she might she could not share her aunt's enthusiasm for their new home, nor her mamma's placid acceptance of her lot.

The small house stifled her, and her thoughts turned more and more to the lovely gracious rooms at Lakesby, to the gardens there and the stables where her dear little mare, Briony, was kept. She had hated leaving Briony, fearful at first how she would be treated by her cousin's grooms, but she was somewhat comforted when Eustace promised that he would keep her entirely for her own convenience. It had altered her opinion of that stern, unsmiling man, when a groom brought Briony over twice a week so that she should not miss her rides, often accompanied by Robert and his pretty wife or his sister Rose. When she saw how well groomed Briony looked she almost forgave Eustace for having inherited Lakesby and could admit that it had not been his fault.

No longer blinded by the position that Lakesby and its estates bestowed upon those who lived there, she began to realize that charming and indulgent as her father had been, he had also been deplorably improvident. While knowing that the Manor must pass at his death to Eustace he had made little provision for his wife and only child, and at his death the sum of three thousand pounds was all that remained to them. All that Eustace could do to increase their slender means, after sparing what furniture they needed for Well Walk and keeping for himself family portraits and large paintings and pieces of furniture that had been especially made for certain rooms, was to suggest that the rest should be sold and the money raised in this way added to the widow's small capital. It was as much as any man in his position could be expected to do, and Allegra did her best to feel grateful, but she possessed a proud, independent spirit, and when the first year at Paragay had slipped into eighteen months and the second February came she felt that she could endure it no longer.

One evening Bell had prepared a little party for whist among their acquaintances in Well Walk, and among the guests was Major Latimer, who was very fond of a game of whist, if not quite so appreciative of the claret that Bell offered as refreshment half-way through the evening.

As Allegra came to replenish his glass he asked her why she was not at the ball in the Assembly Rooms that night, adding with a twinkle that sober card parties were not for pretty young ladies.

Allegra only smiled and did not say that she had been invited to go, not only with her cousins but also with the Tremaynes, and that she had refused both invitations. To attend such balls as Miss Lakesby of Lakesby Manor was one thing, but to attend them as Miss Lakesby of Well Walk was a different matter altogether and her pride would not suffer it for one moment.

'I would rather be a housemaid in one of the great houses of England,' she told herself that evening after their guests had gone, 'than endure another summer here in this poky little house.'

The Times newspaper had been left by the Major for her mother and on the following morning before Mrs Lakesby was down she picked it up idly and glanced through its pages, and turned to the columns advertising for footmen, housekeepers and valets, and between advertisements for an experienced lady's maid and a cook, she saw one for a governess to undertake the care of a girl of six years old. Applicants, it stated, must give satisfactory references as to character and competency, and religion, and should write in the first place to Mrs Glynn, Castle Fetherstone, Fetherstone, Buckinghamshire.

Allegra read it through twice before copying it out and taking the copy to her room. There, at her little writing desk, her heart beating fast, she composed a reply, stating that she was nineteen, a member of the

Church of England, and that although she had no previous experience of teaching, she was the daughter of a gentleman and had been well educated, with a good knowledge of music and French. Excellent references could be supplied if her application should be considered. And she signed herself by her second name, Agnes Lakesby, at Number 14 Well Walk. It was the first time she had cause to be thankful for such an address: she felt it lent an air of genteel poverty to her letter.

The reply came with flattering promptness. Mrs Glynn, it seemed, was the housekeeper at Castle Fetherstone, and she had taken Miss Lakesby's application to Lady Fetherstone, who wished her to say that she would be prepared to consider Miss Lakesby for the post as long as the references she promised were forthcoming. The salary was to be forty pounds a year.

There was only one person to whom she could turn for a reference and she wrote at once to Lady Alicia, asking if she could come and see her on 'business of a strictly private nature'. Her ladyship showed the letter to her husband and asked him what he thought of it.

Mr Tremayne was amused. 'She has probably met some young man who will not be thought to be suitable by the family,' he said.

Lady Alicia did not think that likely. If such a thing had occurred she would have heard about it from Laura Lakesby herself. It was an appeal for help, however, that she could not ignore, and she sent a note to Well Walk to say that she would be calling on Mrs Lakesby the following morning to fetch Allegra to spend the day with Charlotte. It was a long time since they had met and the weather had turned mild for the time of year.

She called, spent a cordial half-hour with Laura and Bell, heard nothing about any unsuitable young men, and in fact there was nothing in either lady's manner to show that she knew anything about Allegra's private business.

As she carried the girl off with her in her little closed carriage she took her hand and said, 'Well, my love? What is this mysterious business about which – I must conclude from their cheerful behaviour this morning – your mamma and aunt know nothing?'

'Oh no, I have not told them. And until it is all settled I do not mean to tell them,' said Allegra, adding a trifle breathlessly, 'The truth is, Lady Alicia, I need a reference.'

'A reference?' Her old friend was puzzled. 'For a servant, do you mean, my dear?'

'Not for a servant, Lady Alicia,' said Allegra, adding desperately, 'For myself.' And before her ladyship could recover from her astonishment she hurried on, 'I have applied for the post of governess at Castle Fetherstone.'

'You have *what*?' Lady Alicia was horrified. 'My dearest child, I don't think I can have heard you aright. You, a Lakesby, wish to take the post of a governess? It is not possible!'

'Oh, Lady Alicia, please do not make it any more difficult than it is already!' Allegra poured out the story of her unhappiness in Paragay, of her dislike for the house, for the town and the people. 'You do not know what it is like to live in Well Walk after Lakesby. I want to push the walls down, I feel that I am imprisoned there, like some female felon!' As her old friend protested against such extravagant talk she went on, 'I know what you are thinking – that it is my pride that is to blame. I should make up my mind to settle down in Paragay and cut out red flannel with the Rector's daughters and flirt with the curates, and the lawyers' sons, and make a close friend of the doctor's wife. But I cannot. They are not of my world.'

'And do you think that the position of governess in a house like Castle Fetherstone would introduce you into a world that was yours?' asked Lady Alicia gravely. 'No, Allegra, I refuse to encourage you in such folly.'

Allegra argued and pleaded in vain, and when they arrived at Mayne Hall and Charlotte was told, she disappointed her by taking sides with her mamma.

'You are talking nonsense, Allegra,' she protested. 'And if you dislike Paragay so much there is a perfect solution ready for you. You must spend long visits with us here at Mayne. Mamma will be delighted to have you as a guest and so will I.' She saw Allegra's expression and laughed. 'You have admitted to Mamma that it is your pride that is at fault and that is very true! You are much too pretty to go out as a governess. Come and look in this mirror and then tell me if you can see yourself as a Miss Stone or a Miss Rawley.' These two severe ladies of uncertain age had been employed at Mayne as Charlotte's governesses in the past, and Allegra's glowing face, with its beautiful dark eyes, long silky lashes and finely marked eyebrows, and the auburn ringlets from under her white silk bonnet brushing the shoulders of her grey silk dress, certainly did not resemble them in the least. In the end she had to laugh too.

She went home disappointed with the result of her visit, however, searching in her mind for some other old friend who would supply the reference she needed and had almost decided on Mrs Willoughby because, in spite of Charlotte's teasing, now that an escape from Paragay had offered itself she meant to take it.

Unexpectedly she found an ally in Mr Tremayne, who, when he heard the whole story after she had gone, gave his opinion that it would do Allegra Lakesby no harm at all to spend a few months in such a position at Castle Fetherstone.

'I was greatly attached to Henry Lakesby,' he said. 'He was a good friend of mine. But he spoiled his family abominably. I know Laura has always been an invalid, but he was for ever buying her new chaises and ponies to draw her round the park, and new sofas to suit her back, and he had special seats made in their carriages when they went to London. He spoiled Allegra too: nothing was too good for her, nothing was denied her. She has had to learn abruptly and painfully that life is not a bed of roses. And to give him his due I do not think Eustace has failed in his duty to his cousin's family, dry old stick as he is.'

Lady Alicia thought it over, a frown between her brows. Then she said, 'One does not like to pry into the intimate affairs of one's friends, but did Henry leave Laura very badly off?'

'Bell has a small income of her own, and I should say that with Laura's it amounts to about two hundred pounds a year. Possibly the sale of the furniture may have given them another twenty.'

'It is not a great deal, Howard.'

'It is very little for people accustomed to a luxurious life. But for those who are prepared to be content with a little, as Laura and Bell are, it should be sufficient, especially as I understand that Eustace has undertaken to pay a number of their expenses and is careful to see that garden produce from the Manor is sent to them regularly. They should manage quite well.'

'But, Allegra –'

'Allegra will not accept it because she is spoiled, my dear. My advice to you is to write that reference for her – Grizelda Fetherstone is a friend of yours – and let her learn for herself that large rooms are not everything, and that money, properly managed, can be an aid to existence and not its aim.'

Lady Alicia would not admit that Allegra had been spoiled. 'She is a dear girl,' she protested. 'And my heart aches for her in that small house surrounded with uncongenial acquaintances. But I will write the reference, though I hope it will not get me into a scrape with Grizel when she learns the truth – as she will sooner or later, no doubt.'

The following morning she called at Number 14 Well Walk early, while Bell was out on the common giving her little dog a run and Paisley was upstairs helping her mistress to dress, and she told Allegra that the letter was written and posted.

'I did not like doing it,' she admitted. 'And it will probably lose me Lady Fetherstone's friendship – I am sure she will not like deception any more than I do. "Agnes" indeed!' And if her ladyship could be so un-dignified as to snort she would have snorted then.

'But Agnes *is* my name. I was christened Allegra Agnes.' Allegra kissed her with affection. 'I am more grateful to you than I can say.'

'You may not be so grateful to me later on,' said Lady Alicia grimly. 'You will not be a welcome guest at Castle Fetherstone, my dear: you will be employed there as a governess, and I think that you cannot know what such a position entails or you would not be so eager to embrace it. There is one thing I must insist upon, however, that you tell your mamma and your aunt what you propose to do without any more delay. Their arguments may influence you where mine cannot.'

At that moment Mrs Lakesby, followed by Paisley laden with shawls, a work-box, two novels and smelling salts, entered the room and was conducted to her usual place on the sofa just as Bell returned from her walk with little Rowley. The ladies greeted their old friend with pleasure and wine and biscuits were offered and declined.

'I am not staying,' she said. 'Allegra has something to tell you.' And with a significant look at that young lady she went out to her carriage.

Thus cornered, Allegra was forced to tell her mamma and her aunt why her ladyship had come and what she proposed to do.

Mrs Lakesby was so horrified that the smelling salts had to be brought into immediate use, but the die was cast and Allegra appeared to treat the matter with an unbecoming cheerfulness. Indeed, the argument that Mrs Lakesby used, that her cousin Eustace would be seriously upset, did not soften her in the least, and when a few days later she received a letter from Lady Fetherstone to say that she had heard from her old friend Lady Alicia Tremayne, who had given Miss Lakesby an excellent reference, and she would be obliged if she would take up her duties at Castle Fetherstone at the end of the month, and she knew that she really was going to leave Paragay behind her, her relief and satisfaction knew no bounds.

She took the letter to one of the benches under the trees that divided the two colonnades and read it again. It was her passport to freedom, and she sat there a little while thinking about Castle Fetherstone and wondering what it was like, and then she walked back slowly to Well Walk. As she reached the steps that led up into the Walk, she saw a gentleman mounting the steps of Mrs Willoughby's house, and while waiting for his knock to be answered he turned to face her. He was tall and broad-shouldered and had black whiskers surrounding a strong jaw that looked as if it with the rest of his face had been tanned by foreign suns, and by comparison his eyes were a deep arresting blue. He was wearing a light-coloured coat and a light hat, unlike the black stove-pipe hats that most gentlemen wore in England, but it was not his dress or his fine physique that drew her attention so much as his eyes that were studying her with interest.

He was a stranger to the Walk and she wondered who he was and what his business could be with Mrs Willoughby when the door was opened and Mrs Willoughby's parlourmaid was there, and as she passed the house Allegra heard her say, 'Oh yes, sir, the mistress is expecting you,' before he entered the house.

Finding her aunt in the dining-parlour, with Paisley helping her to alter a dress for Mrs Lakesby, Allegra asked her if she knew who the stranger could be. 'We all hear a great deal about Mrs Willoughby's grandson in the Navy,' she reminded her, 'but we never hear a word about her son. Could it have been Mr Willoughby, Aunt Bell?'

'Not if he is dark-haired,' said Bell, and then as Paisley left the room with the dress she went on, 'Jack Willoughby is slight and fair, and the reason why we do not hear much about him my love, is because he is an engineer to one of those railway companies, and Mrs Willoughby feels that it has lowered her in the eyes of the Miss Dalrymples. Don't you remember a few evenings ago when the Major referred to Mr George Stephenson, the eldest Miss Dalrymple said quite sharply, "Oh, you mean the railway person, Major." I daresay Mrs Willoughby's visitor is a friend of her son's and in the same way of business.'

'A railway person,' said Allegra smiling, and wondered what the Miss Dalrymples would say when they were told that she had gone out as a governess. She hoped it would not prevent them from including her mamma and her aunt in the circle of their friends.

2

Mrs Lakesby had been right when she said that Eustace and his family would be upset by Allegra's decision. She felt bound to acquaint him with it herself, rather than allow him to learn it from other sources, and she sent a note to the Manor asking him to call on a matter of some importance.

He came the same day, his carriage filling the street and his coachman as usual finding it extremely difficult to turn his horses there.

'Well, Laura?' Eustace said patiently, when Lucy had shown him into the small parlour. 'What is this important matter you wish to consult me about? Is the roof falling in or does the dining-parlour still smoke?'

'It is nothing like that, Eustace.' Laura smiled at him timidly. 'I wish it were something as simple. I would not have sent for you had you not been the head of the family now, and it is a matter that must affect the family as well as myself.'

'Indeed?' Eustace's mind went to his younger brother Barnabas, who was the only member of the family to cause him constant anxiety. He sat down in front of her and regarded her gravely and kindly, his hands on his knees. 'Well, Laura, what is it? Out with it, my dear, and let me judge for myself of its importance.'

'It is Allegra.' She watched his face anxiously. 'I feel that she may listen to you where she will take no heed of me and Bell. The foolish girl has made up her mind to leave Paragay and go out as a governess.'

'A *governess*! *Allegra*!' He echoed the words in astonishment, and then his face darkened with anger.

'You were right to send for me, Laura. She cannot do this.'

'She is using the name of "Agnes" Lakesby, but that is no disguise,' said Laura helplessly. 'It will soon be known who she is – a Lakesby of Lakesby Manor – and what will people think? What will they say?'

'As we shall not know what they think and none of us will give a fig for what they say, such matters are of indifference to me,' he replied with some sharpness. 'Allegra is an extremely pretty girl and no more spoilt than my Rose, and if this were just a whim on her part she would have my blessing. It will do her no harm to be at the beck and call of some fine lady, and I have no doubt she would be back in Paragay before the first week was out, because she is not a young lady to take orders from anyone. But I am afraid that is not the whole of the business, Laura. I think it goes deeper than that, and I will see her at once. I am extremely displeased with her, and I will wait for her in the dining-parlour.'

Poor Mrs Henry began to wish that she had not sent for Eustace at all. She was afraid she had got her darling Allegra into a bad scrape: she had never seen him look so forbidding or so angry.

Allegra was sent for and entered the dining-parlour with a saucy little smile that angered her cousin still further.

'Well, Allegra,' he said sternly, 'your mamma has been telling me about this wild notion of yours, and I would like to hear what you have to say for yourself. You have an astute mind behind that pretty face, and I know exactly what has been passing through it. You think to hold this scheme against me as a threat, so that I shall be forced to increase your mamma's income. That is the root of the matter, is it not? You cannot deny it.'

'But I can and I do!' She flushed crimson and her smile disappeared: her head went up and anger flashed in her eyes. 'You are completely mistaken, and I do not know how you could believe such a thing of me for a moment. We have all we need here, and you have been extremely generous – too generous – to us all.' Did he not keep Briony for her, and as that thought came to her for the first time she wondered who would keep the little mare and ride her when she was away? It was the one thing she had not considered in her plan of escape from Paragay, and as he saw her face change he spoke with more kindness.

'Your mamma brought a fortune of twenty thousand pounds to your father when she married him,' he told her. 'And he had thirty thousand of his own. With the rent roll at Lakesby they should have been able to lead a comfortable existence, and when he died those fortunes should have been left almost intact. But the money was squandered – for I can call it nothing else – down to the last three thousand pounds. I wish I were able to help your mamma more than I can, but there are still debts to be met out of my own pocket, as only the house and estate were entailed to me. Not a penny came with it. And until we have been as Lakesby for a few years we cannot afford to be generous with what is not our own. The estate debts must be settled before anything else, and I do not see how I can do more for your mamma than I am doing now.'

'Nobody could expect it of you.' Allegra felt her eyes filling with tears and she brushed them away angrily. She could not expect her cousin to understand how she felt about Well Walk and Paragay. 'Cousin Eustace, do not be angry with me when I say it is only a desire on my part to escape.'

'To escape? But from what?'

'From these surroundings, from this house, from this gossiping little town.'

'In other words, my dear, you refuse to accept that which my cousins Laura and Bell have accepted without rancour and with a great deal of cheerfulness? Things are forced upon us all against our will from time to time, and I cannot see any happiness for you in a menial position in a great house like Castle Fetherstone.'

'But allow me to find that out for myself,' she pleaded, and he could not resist the appeal in the dark eyes.

'Very well,' he said. 'You shall have your way – and you need have no fears about Briony. She shall be well cared for in your absence.'

She thanked him from her heart and he let her go and went back to the parlour to advise Laura to let her go.

'I am doubtful if she will carry out her intention when the time comes for her to part with you,' he said before he went. 'And if she does it will not be for long. She has yet to learn the ways of these great folk, and Lady Fetherstone has never been one to consider the feelings of others, even those of her personal friends. And now I must go. My brother Barnabas is visiting us, and he is to go pigeon-shooting this morning, and as he is no hand with a gun I trust I shall not find on my return that he has shot my head gamekeeper!'

He left her feeling somewhat comforted. It was a good thing, she thought, that it had been Eustace and not Barnabas who had inherited Lakesby: dearest Henry had not liked Barnabas at all, maintaining that he was not to be trusted. She was surprised, however, when a few days later Barnabas Lakesby called on her on his way back to London.

If he was a scamp, he was a good-looking one, and he had a charm of manner that made him popular with women wherever he went. He greeted Mrs Henry with compliments on her looks, telling her that she was as pretty as ever, and on her dress.

'I like those blue ribbons in your cap,' he said. 'They match your eyes, Laura, my dear, and I'll wager you know it. You were always a pretty woman, and Henry was in luck when he married you.' He took her hand, stroking it gently before he let it go. 'I understand you sent for Eustace a few mornings ago? I trust there is nothing wrong?'

She saw no reason why she should not tell him why she had sent for his brother. The whole neighbourhood must know about it soon if Allegra persisted in her headstrong way. He heard of the plan for her to go out as a governess with dismay.

'Impossible!' he cried. 'Oh my poor Laura, what a terrible thing. But did Eustace do nothing to prevent it?'

'He spoke to her very seriously, but I am afraid her mind is quite made up and he told me that he thought the best thing I could do is to let her have her way. He was sure that she would be home by the end of the first week – if she goes at all.'

'I do not see how he could have treated the matter so lightly.' Barnabas was still indignant. 'Eustace has as much feeling as a fish. But my dearest Laura, why is Allegra doing this? Forgive me if I am impertinent, but can it be because you cannot afford to keep her at home?'

'Oh no, it is nothing like that. It is not lack of means that is making the child unhappy. She says that she cannot forget the larger rooms and the beautiful grounds of Lakesby, and it has made her take a dislike to Paragay, although Bell and I have found it very agreeable here in Well Walk.'

'The house is very poky though, is it not? My

sympathies must be with Allegra there, and I wish with all my heart that you had a better one. There is the Grange now, that would suit you splendidly. I wish I could buy it for you, but I never seem to have any money: it slips through my pockets as if they were lined with mutton fat!' He smiled at her disarmingly. 'I suppose your lawyer would not consider investing your capital in railway shares? They are all the rage now, and there are several small companies in which I have an interest, which would yield you a much better income than you are receiving now. I conclude that Mr Cruikshank has invested your money in the usual five per cents?'

'He would never consent to invest any of it in railway shares.' Laura was quite decided about that. 'Mr Cruikshank detests railways and refuses to have any dealings with them.'

'Then there is no use mentioning such a course of action to him,' said Barnabas cheerfully. 'But Eustace was telling me I think that you have some other assets – a property left to you by your mamma, Lady Kenworthy?'

'You mean my little property in Norfolk – or is it Suffolk? I forget. I think it was near Beccles, but it may have been Yarmouth. Dear Henry went to look at it soon after Mamma's death and he said it was nothing but a ruinous old mansion and forty acres of scrubland that was of no value to anybody. Mr Cruikshank let the house for me for a time, but the last tenants left without paying any rent and it is now in a shocking condition, so I have been told.'

'What is the name of the property?'

'Masterson's. I have never been there in my life, but I think it may have been near Beccles, now I come to think of it, because Henry stayed with his sister, dearest Marianne, when he went to look at it for me, and she lived somewhere near there. She died not long afterwards – the north-east coast was too much for her delicate constitution – but her husband would not listen to anything that Henry said. My darling Allegra inherits her lovely auburn hair, but not her frailty fortunately. I remember Henry saying that Masterson's was a very bleak, barren sort of country. It is a great pity that it was not near Lakesby.'

'It is indeed.' He told her that he would make enquiries about the property the next time he was in that part of the country, which might be within the next few weeks as he was interested in a railway company that had been formed with head offices in Ipswich. 'I might discover some farmer who would be willing to take the place off your hands for several hundred pounds. That would be better than nothing.' He kissed her goodbye, told her to keep a good heart, and begged her to tell his cousin Allegra that he absolutely forbade her to take herself off as a governess. He then continued his way to the railway station in the Lakesby carriage that had brought him there, stopping on the way to call on Mr Cruikshank in Market Square.

Laura passed on his message to Allegra, who put her head in the air and wondered what business it was of Cousin Barnabas. 'Robert told me the last time we were out riding,' she added, 'that he had only come to Lakesby to borrow money from Cousin Eustace. He is always having to pay his debts to save him from bankruptcy, and now that he is taken with this railway mania he is worse than ever.'

A week later she went riding for the last time, and her three cousins accompanied her, Elaine and Rose adding their persuasions to Robert's that she should think better of her decision and cancel her plans for Fetherstone. This she steadfastly refused to do, and as they parted in Well Walk Robert said he would be at the railway station on the morning she was to leave to escort her on the journey.

'I have told him that he must, Allegra,' said Elaine as she protested. 'You have no maid to travel with you, and you cannot go alone '

'Who has ever heard of a governess travelling with her own maid?' said Allegra laughing. She stroked Briony's nose for the last time, before dropping a kiss on it. 'Darling Briony!' she said. 'It is good of your father to keep her for me, Robert.'

'Oh,' said Robert carelessly, 'I daresay she will be more in my stables than in his. She is just right for Elaine – Rose is too heavy for her.'

Rose protested and Elaine laughed and they parted with affection, if still without approval for what Allegra proposed to do.

But Allegra was only nineteen and romance still figured largely in her dreams: she knew exactly what the hero of those dreams must be like. Tall and handsome and with charming manners, he would treat women as if they were princesses, as precious as porcelain, to be cherished and put on pedestals.

The present Lord Fetherstone was young: he was to come of age that summer, and it was his mother who had engaged her as a governess to his sister Susanna. Allegra wondered what he would be like and when she would meet him, and with her head still filled with romantic aspirations on the day before she left Paragay she had an early supper and went off happily to bed.

3

Although she had expected to feel regret when the time came for her to leave Paragay, all that Allegra could experience as her aunt checked through the contents of her small portmanteau with the list in her hand that first morning in March was a sense of utter relief.

No longer would she wake every morning to look out on this stupid street and the heavily curtained windows opposite. There would be instead the extensive grounds of a fine mansion to feast her eyes on and only a gardener perhaps in sight. Or young Lord Fetherstone making a leisured way across the lawns.

'I think you have everything you need.' Bell straightened her back after stooping over the trunk and slipped the list under the crossed tapes in the lid. 'You must remove this list after you have unpacked and keep it by you. I daresay your trunk may be stored in some distant boxroom where you will not be able to reach it easily.'

'I daresay it will.' The plain straw bonnet and brown stuff dress that Allegra had selected as being suitable for a governess, ugly as they were, made her look even prettier, Bell thought, and she sighed as she remembered the ball dresses locked away in the cupboard behind her.

'You will write frequently, will you not, my love?' she said anxiously. 'And none of your niminy-piminy letters either!' and then as Allegra laughed she went on seriously, 'I am so afraid the servants will be familiar, taking advantage of your position there, and that your feelings may be lacerated every hour of the day.' Bell was always talking of feelings being lacerated and Allegra laughed again.

'My feelings will only be of gladness because I have exchanged this horrid little house for Fetherstone,' she declared. 'And gladness for you too, because your burden will be lightened by having one less mouth to feed, and a hungry one at that. I have tried not to give rein to my appetite, Aunt Bell dearest, but I do seem to eat a great deal.'

'You have a healthy appetite, my love, and there is plenty of food to satisfy it here. We are not paupers.'

'I know, but when I am gone Mamma will be able to have more of the things she fancies. An invalid needs dainty fare and a bottle of good wine now and again. There are no cellars here to turn to and no obliging Ratcliffe to fetch a bottle of port wine for Mamma.' Their butler Ratcliffe had been house steward as well at Lakesby, and was there now, looking after Eustace's wines as carefully, no doubt, as he had looked after his cousin Henry's. 'And I am not sure, Aunt Bell,' went on Allegra, with a sigh for the absent Ratcliffe, 'if the claret you have ordered from the wine merchant lately has been as good as that of Lakesby.'

'It is a very good claret, dear, or so the salesman told me.' Bell sounded a trifle uncertain. 'Not that I know a great deal about wines. Ladies usually leave that sort of thing to their butlers. I wonder how Ratcliffe is progressing with his new master?'

'I am sure you need not be concerned about him, any more than you need be anxious about me,' said Allegra composedly. 'Lady Alicia says that Lady Fetherstone is not in the least formidable, although she likes to have her own way.'

'No doubt she does. I expect she is a very fine lady, and that she will treat you as – a governess.'

'I cannot see why that should present any terrors for

me. My governesses were not treated badly, in fact they were always considered to be members of our family.'

If Bell thought that a country house like Lakesby Manor had a warm and friendly atmosphere that might be totally lacking in the far grander mansion to which her niece was going, she did not say so. She reminded her that Lady Alicia had also told them that Lord Fetherstone was a handsome young man and deplorably susceptible where young ladies were concerned.

'Then perhaps as he will not regard me as a young lady but only as a governess I shall be free from his attentions,' said Allegra light-heartedly.

'You may not be – for that very reason.'

'Oh, my dearest Aunt!' Allegra gave her a hug. 'It is unlike you to look on the dark side of things. I promise that I shall not allow the young gentleman to seduce me – if I ever meet him – and that I shall lock my bedroom door at night.'

Her aunt laughed with her, and then glancing out of the window and seeing an old man with a barrow stop in the street below she said, 'There is old Lucky to fetch your portmanteau to the railway station.' Lucky was an ancient gentleman who combined the duties of outside porter at the station with those of a general messenger. 'I will call Lucy to help me to do up these straps and then Lucky can carry your trunk downstairs.'

As the little maid came running up to help with the portmanteau straps Allegra went to say goodbye to her mamma. 'There is no hurry,' she told her aunt. 'Lucky thinks I am travelling on the first-class train, but the second class leaves half an hour later.'

She went to her mother's room and was embraced tenderly, Laura making her promise that if she should be unhappy at Castle Fetherstone she would write to her at once.

'Robert will come and fetch you,' she promised her.

'Or Eustace. I daresay they will not like it overmuch, but they will do it for me. They are very kind men, both Robert and his father.'

Allegra gave the required promise and went away downstairs to the little passage that passed for a hall, where her aunt was waiting in bonnet and shawl ready to walk with her behind Lucky and his cart to the railway station. Rather unkindly, Allegra hoped the Miss Dalrymples saw them as they passed.

'Mamma was remarkably cheerful,' she said brightly as they set out. 'I am so glad.' She had expected tears and they had not been shed, and she would not acknowledge that the lack of feeling on her dear mamma's part had hurt her a little.

'Yes,' said Bell, equally cheerful now that the time for her niece's departure had come. 'She has taken it with remarkable fortitude.' She did not add that Eustace's opinion that Allegra would be back in Paragay at the end of a week had done much to raise their spirits.

A cold north-east wind met them as they turned the corner of Well Walk into Market Street, but the sun was shining and in the sky woolly clouds moved fast across the blue as if they were playing a game of catch-as-catch-can. The wind was in a playful mood too, whipping the stove-pipe hats from old gentlemen's heads and blowing ladies' skirts about with an indecent abandon.

Paragay was proud of its railway station. It was a small classical building, built in the Italianate style of brick and stone: its coupled, round-headed windows and pinnacled turrets Florentine in appearance. When the two ladies arrived breathless after their battle with the wind they found that the first-class train was not yet in, much to Bell's relief.

'Now there is no excuse,' she said. 'You *shall* travel

first class!' And brushing aside her niece's protests she left her to walk on to the platform where old Lucky was standing guard over her portmanteau, and made her way to the booking office, where, however, she found Robert waiting for her, the tickets in his hand and looking put out.

'Oh there you are, Cousin Bell!' he said. 'I was afraid Allegra would miss the train, which would have meant an hour's wait because she is not travelling second class and neither am I. I hope the trains back from Bending Junction to Paragay are hourly too, as I do not wish to spend the entire day waiting on railway stations. Elaine is very anxious over our eldest little boy, and I did not like leaving her. He has a bad throat and a fever.'

Bell expressed her sympathy for Elaine and the little boy and accompanied him on to the platform to join Allegra, where he stared in astonishment and disgust at her bonnet and dress. 'Is that your idea of how a governess should dress?' he demanded. 'Because I never saw one of Rose's make such a guy of herself. Where on earth did you get it Allegra? I do not think I have ever seen you in an uglier dress and bonnet.'

Her appearance had not improved his temper. She was certainly not looking her best, which, she thought with satisfaction, was as it should be. Her hair was strained back under the plain bonnet and dressed in a knot at the nape of her neck, without a ringlet in sight, and the dress was lamentable.

'I found the dress and the bonnet in an old box that had come with some other of our things from Lakesby,' she told him serenely. 'The box was full of old dresses that we kept for dressing up when we played charades with the Tremaynes. When I came across it last week I thought it was just the thing.' She stroked the rough serge of the ugly skirt complacently. 'I am sorry if you do not think it fine enough for a governess.'

'Allegra, you are not playing charades!' His sharp tone rebuked her for her frivolity. 'It is not a game that you are going to play at Castle Fetherstone, and although you say you will have only one little girl to teach I have no doubt she will be spoiled and naughty enough for a dozen.'

She smiled at him consolingly. 'The train will be here in a few minutes, so do not let us quarrel before I go. And I will repeat that there is no need for you to come with me: I would far sooner that you went home and let me go alone.'

'I cannot allow you to travel about the country on your own,' he said frowning. 'If you insist on playing this sort of prank then naturally your relatives must suffer for it.' He looked past her moodily to the station entrance where he had told his groom to wait with his horse in case his cousin should change her mind, and then as a man came out to join the waiting passengers on the platform he gave an exclamation of surprise and pleasure.

'Buckhurst, by all that's holy!' he exclaimed. 'Now I wonder if he is travelling in your direction? Because if he should be going as far as Bending Junction I am sure he would take my place and see that you alighted there and were met by the carriage that you say is to be sent for you.'

Before she could protest he had left her, walking off rapidly, and turning her head she saw him hold out his hand to the same 'railway person' that she had seen enter Mrs Willoughby's house a few weeks previously. The situation was evidently explained to him and she saw the stranger smile and nod his head, and the two men approached her together, Robert's ill-humour gone as he introduced Mrs Willoughby's friend to her.

'Mr Buckhurst came to see me at the Dower House a few weeks back,' he told her. 'He is the engineer for a railway that is planned from Bending Junction to Worcester, and my godfather left me a small property near Worcester that is likely to be required for the line. I recognized him the moment we met, though it must have been thirteen or fourteen years since I last saw you, eh Buckhurst?'

'All of fourteen years, sir.' Mr Buckhurst's speech had a pleasant country burr, and his eyes regarded Allegra with the same intense gaze that she had encountered before. 'I came to see your father in London for his permission, as his cousin's heir, to drive the London to Birmingham railway through some of the Lakesby land.'

'I was a schoolboy then, and I would have given anything to be done with school and working with you. I believe you were under George Stephenson at that time?'

'No, sir. Under his son, Robert Stephenson, who had taken over a hotel in St John's Wood outside London, where he had about thirty draughtsmen producing quantities of drawings. His energy and speed were lessons to any young men.'

'You did not stay with him after the railroad was completed?'

'No. He recommended me to an engineer who was to build a railroad in France, and from there I was asked to be the engineer in charge of a line in North America, and from there to one in Germany, before returning home to work again here. I have made a preliminary survey of the Bending Junction to Worcester line, but we are being held up by some difficulty over the purchase of a few acres of the Fetherstone land. I am on my way to London now to meet Lord Fetherstone and his guardian at our Euston office, and I shall be delighted to accompany Miss Lakesby to Bending Junction.'

The train was now entering the station and Bell took Allegra's hand, telling her to write as soon as she arrived, trying to make herself heard above the noise of the engine. Robert in the meanwhile walked with Mr Buckhurst up the platform, and when the train stopped with a great clanking of carriages he helped Allegra into a carriage that contained one other lady, her companion and a lap-dog, while Buckhurst summoned a porter to lift the small portmanteau on to the roof, where it was lodged securely inside the protecting rail and covered with tarpaulin in case they should run into rain.

Mr Buckhurst settled his companion in a corner seat facing the way they were going, and after she had waved goodbye to her aunt and cousin he sat down opposite her on the same side as the lady's companion, who drew her cashmere dress away in disdain for the brown stuff gown and the gentleman's unfashionable hat before turning her shoulder on them.

The carriage had three seats on either side, upholstered in drab cloth with heavy fringes reaching from the edge of the cushioned seats to the floor. Padded arm-rests divided travellers from each other, and the head-rests extended to the ceiling. The windows were larger and the carriage far less cramped than those in a private carriage, and Allegra expressed herself as being delighted with this new mode of travel.

Her animated face was that of a pleased child as they left the station behind and Mr Buckhurst regarded her with a slightly puzzled expression. Her dress had none of the finery one would expect in the daughter of the late Henry Lakesby, and he wondered if Eustace had struck as hard a bargain with his cousin's widow as he had with the Birmingham to London Company fourteen years ago.

'Are you visiting friends in Bending?' he asked.

She glanced at the lady in the corner, but she was holding up her dog to look out of the window and neither she nor her companion had any interest in their conversation. She smiled and lowered her voice. 'I have taken a position of governess at Castle Fetherstone,' she said, as if she were imparting a dreadful secret, but her eyes were dancing and he found himself smiling in return. She was so young and so full of spirit, and he thought Eustace must have treated her family very shabbily to make such a thing necessary, when, seeing the concern and kindness in his face and the man himself so large and dependable, she told him about her father's death and their move from the Manor to the cramped little house in Well Walk.

'My cousin Eustace has been very kind indeed,' she told him, dispelling his unjust suspicions of the gentleman. 'But Papa was not quite as provident as he should have been, and anything larger than Number 14 Well Walk would have been beyond our means. At first I determined that I would like to live there, but as time went on I found that the small rooms, and the confined atmosphere of the Walk, defeated my good resolutions. I felt that if I could only live in a house like Lakesby Manor again I would not care what I did – what work I undertook to attain that end. I would even be a housemaid in such an establishment, because I would be able to breathe again. So I answered an advertisement for a governess at Castle Fetherstone and I am going there today to take up my duties.'

'And does your family approve of what you are doing?'

'Not at all.' Her smile held defiance but her eyes begged his approval and after a moment he said thoughtfully:

'My father was a wheelwright, and before she married him my mother was a housemaid at the Great House, as we called it in our village. After she married her younger sister took the post she had held there, and when I was a little fellow my mother would take me to see my aunt sometimes, when the housekeeper, a most important lady, permitted it. My aunt was terrified of her. But when she did allow a visit we would enter the house by the back entrance, and what impressed me most was a long, stone-floored passage that led from the servants' quarters to those of the family. At the end of this passage there was a double row of bells, high up on the wall, each with the name of the room to which it was connected painted above it, and beyond those bells there was a door with a weight and pulley attached. That was the door, I was told, that shut off the family's side of the house, and it was always kept closed. The weight and pulley had been fixed to ensure privacy, in case some careless servant forgot to shut it behind him, when it would close of its own accord. I am not sure where a governess's place is in such a household – on which side of the door?'

She looked at him quickly and her smile faded a little. 'I believe you are trying to frighten me,' she said.

'I would not dream of doing such a thing,' he assured her. 'And I am sure you know more about such things than I do.' He began to talk of the gently undulating country through which they were now passing, drawing her attention to the many beechwoods.

'Buckinghamshire is noted for its beeches,' he told her. 'Bending Junction's only occupation was that of furniture making before the railway came, and it is still, in spite of it.'

He went on to tell her of the difficulties that he had encountered in the making of the railway on which they were travelling, and she found it absorbing, and even more so the account of his adventures abroad. The contractor for a railway in France had once told him that the gangs of navvies he had taken with him had filled the French people with astonishment. While saying that they had never met with such packs of barbarians they also acknowledged that they had never seen men work so hard.

'Does the contractor of a railway choose his gangs of workmen then, sir?'

'Oh yes. He is responsible for everything, tools, wagons, men and latterly even for selecting the railway's engineer.' There was a wry twist to his smile. 'These railroad contractors are very great men, and very wealthy too. I have been fortunate in working for a gentleman by the name of Thomas Brassey, which will mean nothing to a young lady like yourself. But he is an influential railway engineering contractor. He employed me abroad, and recently asked me to be the engineer for the construction of this new branch line between Bending Junction and Worcester.'

'Mamma owns some land in Suffolk,' she said thoughtfully. 'Or is it Norfolk? I wish it could be sold to a railway company as it is useless for anything else, but nobody appears to want it.'

'Where is it situated?'

'Somewhere near Beccles, I have been told, but Mamma has never been there and does not know a great deal about it.'

'If a railway had wanted the land they would have approached her by this time.' He went on to talk of other things and the time passed so quickly that when the train stopped at Bending Junction before going on to London Allegra could scarcely believe that an hour and a half had passed since they left Paragay fifty miles away.

The Junction, she saw at first glance, was an infinitely superior structure to that at Paragay. With its battlements it resembled a castle more than a place for the

38

arrival and departure of trains, and there were two platforms, where Paragay only had one. The platforms, one on either side of the London line, were joined by a glass roof upheld by iron pillars set at intervals down the edge of each platform, and beyond the station the line split into two, one curving away towards the east and the other continuing to London.

Mr Buckhurst assisted his young companion to alight from the carriage and summoned a porter to fetch her portmanteau from the roof, and then went outside with her into the station entrance, where a small and rather shabby carriage was waiting with a pair of horses in its shafts. If it had not been for the coachman's livery Allegra would not have associated it with Fetherstone at all, but as she came out with Mr Buckhurst beside her, followed by the porter with the portmanteau, a young groom in the same livery who had been holding the horses' heads came over to greet her with a slightly cheeky grin, and without even touching his hat asked if she might be the new governess for Castle Fetherstone.

She was so taken aback by the man's familiarity that for a moment she could not answer and left it to Mr Buckhurst to inform him that she was Miss Lakesby. 'I believe the young lady is expected,' he added. 'Be so good as to take her portmanteau.'

'Oh yes, sir. Very good, sir.' The groom touched his hat to the engineer and hurried to relieve the porter of the small portmanteau, disposing of it quickly on the carriage roof. Then he opened the door and let down the steps for Allegra, the grin gone from his face.

'So here you are at your journey's end,' said Mr Buckhurst, taking the hand she held out to him, and she thought she saw a faint amusement in his face. 'It is not my habit to visit castle folk, Miss Lakesby, but if we obtain Lord Fetherstone's permission to run the railway through his land perhaps I may see you in the village sometimes with your charge.'

'Perhaps you may, sir.' Already annoyed by the cheeky groom and the shabbiness of the conveyance that had been sent for her, she thanked him coolly for his help on the journey and mounted the step with a dignity that would have done justice to the elder Miss Dalrymple.

As she glanced back she saw his striding off towards the London train without another glance in her direction, and she wished then that she had been more grateful, because in spite of her brave words to him and to her family, she was setting out to a country unknown to her and a life of which she had no experience whatever, and this was emphasized as the carriage moved off and she found that she had a companion for the last part of her journey.

4

A large lady was already seated in the little carriage and the bundles she was clutching, combined with her bulk, left very little room for Allegra.

' 'Ope I'm not crowding of you, dear,' she said cheerfully.

Allegra said that she had enough room and asked if she was Mrs Glynn.

'The housekeeper?' The large lady burst into fits of laughter, shaking all over and gasping for breath. 'Lor' bless you, dear,' she said when she was able to speak, 'don't you ever let Mrs Glynn 'ear you say a thing like that! Me, Polly Growse, 'ousekeeper at Castle Fetherstone! That's a good 'un, that is. One of the sewing maids I was, till I left to get wed, and Mrs Glynn still sends for me when she's 'ard-pressed. Terrible lot of mending and patching of linen up there. Not linen used by the family o' course. Nuffin' but the best for lords and such. But the nursery and the schoolroom and the ladies' maids all has to do with patches and darns. One person what wouldn't 'ave it was the late governess, Miss Scrimger. The fust time there was a patched tablecloth on the schoolroom table she goes and sees Mrs Glynn straight away. "Mrs Glynn," she says, very grand-like, " 'ow do you expect me to bring my charges up as young ladies when you give 'em tablecloths as is only fit for the servants' 'all?" Nobody else would have dared to speak to Mrs Glynn like that — we was all frit out of our lives at her. But that Miss Scrimger didn't 'alf give 'erself airs. Well, you see, she'd been 'ead governess in a duke's 'ouse'old, so she would be 'igh and mighty, wouldn't she?'

41

Allegra agreed, her heart sinking a little. There was nothing, she felt, at all high and mighty about herself, and she foresaw patched and darned tablecloths gracing the schoolroom table at every meal. But she supposed she would only have meals there with Susanna when her ladyship was from home. When she was in residence they would dine with her downstairs.

Her companion was a garrulous lady and although she did not encourage her Allegra soon learned something about the house where she was to be governess.

There were nearly forty indoor servants, she was told, and about as many again outside.

' 'Im,' her companion said, nodding at the coachman's back, ' 'e's the under coachman, Briggs. Mostly 'e drives the luggage brake to the station to fetch visitors' luggage, and a number of journeys 'e has to make of it at times, I kin tell you. The groom, Bert, 'e's a bit cheeky, but 'e don't mean no 'arm. A good lad is Bert, and wunnerful with 'osses. He's need to be too. There's stabling up there for nigh on fifty 'osses and there's times when I've been there and every stall 'as been filled. Maybe those times will come agin when 'is lordship comes of age. 'Er leddyship now, she's just a shavin' on the close side, if you take my meaning. Won't spend a penny where a ha'penny will do. She likes living in Lunnun better'n Fetherstone and always did.'

The road now entered a deep plantation of beeches, the branches meeting overhead for the best part of a mile, and Mrs Growse said she was only going as far as the village because she had a daughter married to one of the estate carpenters, and as the poor soul was expecting her first it was only right that her mother should be there.

'Castle Fetherstone stands up on a hill some way out from the village.' she went on. 'You'll catch a glimpse of it soon as we come out of these here trees.'

And as the road left the trees behind Allegra saw the enormous mansion for the first time. It had been built on the southern slopes of a small range of hills, looking across a lovely valley to where more beechwoods climbed more hills almost to the top. She wondered why the house had been called a castle, because its only likeness to such antiquity was in the east and west wings that had been built in the form of large square towers, castellated in the Gothic style so popular in the previous century.

'When the family is in residence,' Mrs Growse told her, 'the flag flies from the mast in the west tower.' Allegra asked if any of the family were expected there soon.

'Lor' bless you no, my dear. 'Er leddyship and the young ladies is in Lunnun for the season and you won't see none of 'em I don't suppose until 'is lordship comes of age in July. We'm going to see some rare old junketing then, I promise you. I don't s'pose you've ever seen nothin' like it in your life.'

The village came in view, its cottages a picturesque jumble of half-timber, plaster, flint and old brickwork, clustered round a Norman church. In the main street there was a small inn with a sign, 'The Pewter Pot', hanging above it, a smithy, a bakery, a haberdasher's and a butcher's shop. A much more imposing inn, 'The Fetherstone Arms', faced on to a green with a duckpond nearer the church, and the Dower House with the Rectory next door, stood back behind large gardens just beyond the churchyard. Opposite these imposing residences was a row of small cottages with neatly kept gardens, and at the gate of one of them a young man was standing, anxiously watching for the carriage.

'Looks like as if the poor wench has started,' said Mrs Growse. She waved to her son-in-law, who came hurrying to help her out of the carriage.

43

'I hope all goes well,' said Allegra, as she handed out her bundles.

'Niver can tell with the fust one, dear,' said Mrs Growse, adding cheerfully that it was no use meeting trouble half-way. The door was slammed shut by the young groom and the carriage moved on, and as they drew nearer to the great house the size of it continued to surprise Allegra.

A long winding road led up to a Gothic arch flanked by lodges half-way up the hill. This was the main entrance, and here they stopped for the gates to be opened. The lodge-keeper, instead of touching his hat to her, merely stared at Allegra with some curiosity, while exchanging a word or two with Briggs before they went on. She wondered if, like Bert, he did not consider a governess to be worthy of a touched hat.

Beyond the arch the road continued through parkland studded with clumps of trees and after a while turned right, leaving a large stable block on the left as it approached the carriage sweep before the imposing north front of the mansion. Before they could reach it, however, Briggs turned his horses to the left and the carriage stopped outside a side entrance in the east wing. The groom opened the door and let down the steps and took her portmanteau as far as this entrance before the carriage started back towards the stables.

A stern-looking lady dressed in black silk with a lace cap was waiting at the side door to receive her and she guessed her to be the redoubtable Mrs Glynn of whom Mrs Growse had spoken with such awe.

Allegra found nothing terrifying about her. In the old days when as a little girl she had been taken by her parents to visit friends and relatives in large country houses there were always such severe-looking ladies in the same black silk and lace caps waiting at the top of main staircases to conduct them to their rooms.

She smiled and held out her hand. 'I think you must be Mrs Glynn?' she said. 'I am the new governess, Miss Lakesby.'

'To be sure.' The housekeeper's grasp was warm and friendly. 'If you will follow me, Miss Lakesby, I will show you to your room. I hope you had a pleasant journey?'

'Yes, thank you.' The east door led into a small square hall paved with flagstones. From it a fair-sized staircase led upwards, but Allegra was conducted past these stairs and through a door that led on to a much humbler flight – or rather three flights in all. At the top of the third flight she was led down a passage to her room, a pleasant if rather small apartment looking towards the stable block, in the centre of which was a clock, painted blue, with brass hands that caught the late-afternoon sun.

'The nursery footman will bring your box to you, Miss Lakesby,' said Mrs Glynn. 'And when you have removed your bonnet the door to the schoolroom and nursery quarters is to the left at the end of this corridor. Miss Susanna and Mrs Capper are waiting for you there.'

'Thank you, Mrs Glynn. I will be as quick as I can.' But after the housekeeper had departed with a great rustling of the silk dress Allegra put her head out of the bedroom door and looked down the passage to the other door, firmly shut, and was relieved to see that it had no weight or pulley attached. The nursery footman appearing at that moment at the top of the stairs with her portmanteau she went back into her room and removed her bonnet and mantle, glancing round at her room with a wry amusement. The furniture was of the plainest description, and on the scrubbed floor was one faded rug beside the bed. There was only one chair, a small mirror hanging on the wall, a shabby wooden wash-hand stand and one cupboard for her clothes, but obviously a governess was not expected to possess many gowns. She could not think that the mighty Miss Scrimger had been offered such accommodation.

She smoothed her hair in front of the small mirror, washed her face and hands at the wash-hand stand to take away the dirt from the train smoke, and went down the passage and opened the door.

On the other side she immediately found herself in a different world. Here there was a thick carpet on the floor and the doors that led off the square landing were of mahogany, and led into large rooms. She caught sight of Susanna's bedroom with a chintz-hung bed and a lace coverlet with knots of pink ribbons. Chintz curtains were at the windows and there was a rose-pink carpet on the floor, reminding her of the room she had as a child at Lakesby. Of the nurseries only the day nursery remained, the schoolroom being next door, and it was in the day nursery that Susanna was watching for her, with her old nurse, Mrs Capper, behind her.

Susanna was a pretty little fair-haired girl and from the moment of meeting her Allegra knew that she would be able to manage her. The child was polite and well mannered and showed her the lesson books she had and what she had been learning, and seemed eager to like her. Her heart lifted as she sat at her solitary cold supper of meat and small beer and bread and cheese after the child had been taken off to bed by Mrs Capper that night, and when she had finished she went to her room and unpacked her clothes before slipping into bed herself.

Mrs Capper, in the meantime, after Susanna was asleep, went down to the housekeeper's parlour as she usually did when the family were not in residence, to have a chat over a glass of port before going to bed herself, and they discussed the new governess with kindliness if with some misgiving.

'She's a lady,' said Mrs Glynn. 'You can tell that at once from the way she speaks, gentle, and treating you as an equal as real gentlefolk do. Directly she saw me she put out her hand to me, which was more than that Miss Scrimger ever did.'

'She is not accustomed to waiting on others, though,' said Mrs Capper. 'I don't know how she will go on here, I'm sure. Governesses is governesses, all said and done.'

'There's only one thing against her as far's as I can see,' said Mrs Glynn regretfully. 'She is far too pretty to be a governess.' After a moment she added, 'I wonder she didn't turn all the heads of the young gentlemen in Paragay.'

'There's one young gentleman I know of whose head might be turned by her, easily,' said Mrs Capper, and her eyes met those of the housekeeper meaningly.

'I've not heard that his lordship will be at Fetherstone in the summer,' said Mrs Glynn. 'And when he does pay us a visit I daresay it will be only on account of this here railway.'

'Which I hope will keep his lordship too occupied to notice Miss Susanna's new governess,' said Mrs Capper.

'I hope so too,' said Mrs Glynn, but she did not sound too sure as she poured out a second glass of port.

.   .   .   .   .

As the train had carried Mr Buckhurst on to London he found his thoughts dwelling pleasantly for a time on Miss Lakesby. She was a pretty child, almost prettier without the auburn ringlets that he had noticed when he first saw her coming up the steps into Well Walk, her bright hair neatly braided now under the straw bonnet. He wondered what Robert Lakesby had been about, to hand her over so casually to the keeping of a man he had only met twice in his life. It showed a complete disregard for his cousin's safety.

From Allegra his thoughts went back to his own boyhood. He had always been fond of drawing: a piece of slate and a bit of chalk would keep him happy for hours as a child, and as he grew older he would beg a sheet of paper and a stump of a pencil from his aunt at the Great House. His father had paid a penny a week for him to learn his letters at the dame's school in the village, and in between that and learning the wheelwright's trade he would work out designs for wheels and spokes and axles and brakes that might be worked by machinery. A newspaper containing a design for an engine that had been supplied to a North Country mill and caused trouble among the work-people there before they smashed it, had been thrown into a waste-paper basket at the Great House and his aunt kept it for him to study. He discussed it that night with his father and showed a great deal more understanding of the engine than John Buckhurst, who declared, not without reason, that things made by hand were far better and lasted longer than any turned out by new-fangled machinery, which was to his mind the work of the devil.

Young William, however, found an unexpected champion in the parson, old Mr Walters, who brought his gig in one day to have the off-wheel axle mended, and caught sight of the lad at the work bench under the window, poring over the drawings of the machinery for the mill. Beside him there was the precious spread of an old paper bag, with his own drawings on it, attempting to illustrate the use of similar machinery in a wheelwright's shop.

While he was waiting for his gig, Mr Walters bent over the drawings with the lad, glancing at him shrewdly over his spectacles. 'You did this?' he asked, pointing to the paper bag, and when William nodded he said sharply, 'Buckhurst, let me have this boy of yours on evenings when he is not wanted here. I believe I could make something of him.'

'You mean all that there machinery he's so taken with, sir? Work of the devil I call it, Parson.'

'It may not be. It could be of great benefit to many people in the future, if anything comes of these engines they are trying to run on wheels. The lad's taught himself draughtmanship, but he will need mathematics and instruction on how to put his ideas into words. Can you read, boy?'

'Dame Brewster learned him,' said Buckhurst surlily.

'And can you write, boy?'

'I print the words from the newspaper, sir.'

'That's no good. You've to learn to write clearly and in an educated hand. I shall expect you tonight, boy, if your father can spare you, and don't keep me waiting.'

'I won't, sir.' And so his evenings with the old gentleman began. He learned all that he could teach him with avidity, anxious to discover more about machinery that could do so much more than man, and when the Stockton to Darlington Railway was opened in 1825 he and his old friend were as excited as if they had been the inventors instead of Stephenson.

When the old man died in the following year it was found that he had left sufficient money for the twelve-year-old lad to attend the Grammar School in the town five miles away. He walked the ten miles happily every day, and his father let him go grudgingly, saying that he would never make a wheelwright in any case – he had not the patience.

'You're in sich a 'urry to git things done,' he said. 'You need time and trouble to turn spokes for an axle, to fit 'em into it, to make a rim to take 'em. You'll niver do them things by your machinery. It's devil's work, is that.'

But by the time he was sixteen an opportunity presented itself for William to take a position as draughtsman under Robert Stephenson and at eighteen he was present at the opening the Liverpool and Manchester Railway by the Duke of Wellington. Even the tragic accident that marred that opening failed to make him agree with his father that it was devil's work, and soon afterwards he was working once more under Robert on the London–Birmingham line.

It was during those years that he met Mr Henry Lakesby and his heir Eustace, having been sent, young as he was, to explain the plan of the railway where it touched the Lakesby land. He thought of all the things he had done since, all the railways he had worked on, the countries he had seen, the men he had worked with, until today when at thirty-four he was a recognized engineer in his own right with a comfortable fortune behind him.

5

Julian Armitage could see that his ward's mamma was in a temper when he walked into her drawing-room in Eaton Square. Lady Fetherstone's two elder daughters Augusta and Sarah, demurely working at their netting in one of the windows that overlooked the square, cast him a look of amused despair behind her back. They were pretty girls, dressed in silk dresses that became them, rose-red for dark-haired Sarah, and ice-blue for fair-haired Augusta, their tiny waists accentuated by the fullness of their taffeta skirts.

'I am absolutely furious,' her ladyship declared, rising from her chair as if impelled by a spring. 'I sent for you, Julian, because I wish you to do something at once to stop these abominable railway people from taking their horrid line through our land. The girls will bear me out when I say that I am not alone in my disgust. All my relations and friends are quite horrified. Let the railway be taken through the Spender property on the far side of Copley hills: it shall not be allowed to desecrate our lovely meadows and spoil my view across the valley. You must put your foot down and refuse to have anything to do with it.' She paused, regarding her old friend with a sparkling eye. 'You are not listening to me!'

'Indeed I am, ma'am.' But Mr Armitage's face registered nothing but amusement and her ladyship could have boxed his ears. Nobody could call Julian Armitage a good-looking man, but there was a strength of character in his square jaw and slightly Roman nose that inspired trust, which was why he had been selected for Oliver's guardian. He had not failed in that trust either, though he was apt to complain that his hair and whiskers had gone prematurely white under the strain.

'You are as bad as Oliver!' Lady Fetherstone cried. 'You encourage him in his disregard for my feelings. I do not think either of you give a fig for Castle Fetherstone or the estate.'

'On the contrary, I have a great deal of respect for your feelings and for Castle Fetherstone, Grizel.' Had he not known her in the days when she was Lady Grizelda Shane, before she met Lord Fetherstone? But the amusement was still there in his face.

'You may make a joke of it.' There was no abatement of her energy. 'But it will be an abomination if this railway comes to Fetherstone. Not only for us – I daresay we should tolerate our spoiled view in time – but the Rector tells me the village is up in arms about it. They are really terrified at the thought of gangs of navvies rampaging through the village at night, and as there is an alternative route planned through the Spender land I do not see why it cannot go that way.'

'I am sure Sir Giles Spender would be delighted to sell some of his land to the company, my dear, but Oliver would also be pleased to sell his. I am his guardian only until he reaches the age of twenty-one, we are now in March and that date is only four months away. I can advise him but I cannot consent to, or refuse, a project over his head. He must now be consulted in everything as a responsible young man, aware of his duty to his estates.'

'Oliver is opinionated enough already without your encouragement,' said young Lord Fetherstone's mamma in mortified tones. 'I am sure when I was a girl young men did not air their views so freely.'

'I daresay they did, but you did not hear them.'

'We told you, Mamma, that Uncle Julian would take Oliver's part,' said Augusta with a saucy smile for her brother's guardian.

'I am taking nobody's part,' he said impatiently. 'But I have been pleased to see that Oliver is developing an interest in the estates that have passed to him, not only at Fetherstone but in Yorkshire as well. He is anxious to do all he can for his tenants: since he came down from Oxford at the end of last summer he has made it his business to consult Duffy frequently, as well as to visit Yorkshire, and consult his agent there, to see his tenants personally and to listen to their complaints, promising to do all he can to meet them. He has an excellent agent in Duffy at Fetherstone, who has also been most encouraged by his attitude and interest.'

'It seems he will listen to his agents far more readily than he will listen to his mother,' said Lady Fetherstone angrily. 'My dearest Edmund used to say that all farmers grumble: it is a habit bred of the English climate. And where will Oliver obtain the money to fulfil all his promises?'

'From the proposed railway. Yes, Grizel, you may exclaim and the girls may laugh, but the company is prepared to pay handsomely for the privilege of running five miles of track through the Fetherstone land. It will disrupt the village more than it will Castle Fetherstone: there is a bridge to be built over the river before it skirts Horseshoe Hill, but that will be to the east of the house and you will see nothing of it.' The range of hills on which Castle Fetherstone stood was shaped in a rough horseshoe, hence its name. 'Oliver is very pleased with it.'

'Oliver is all for progress,' said his sister Sarah.

'Progress!' cried her mamma. 'Does he imagine that hideous railways scarring the face of England and spoiling acres of beautiful landscape can be called progress?'

'If he does he is not alone in his opinion.' Mr Armitage held up his hand to check her protest. 'No, you must hear me out. In July Oliver will be free to run a railway through his park and have a station built at the lodge gates, and nobody will be able to stop him.'

'I do not know why Edmund ever thought you could be a help to me or to my eldest son. The loss of my privacy evidently means nothing to you.'

'It is sheer nonsense to say that your privacy will be threatened, my dear. The track is to run at the foot of the Copley hills, at least three or four miles away. It will be on the other side of the river, and your house is well screened by trees. The most you could see would be an occasional puff of smoke if you climbed to the top of the flagstaff, and I do not think you are likely to do that. The villagers have my sympathies, I own, because the disadvantages of building a railway is undoubtedly the spoilation of villages and small towns. That is why I have arranged to meet the engineer of the company tomorrow so that I can make a stand to protect Fetherstone village before any permission is given. There are no railway cottages or huts to be built there, nor any colony of tents to house these rough railway fellows. I give you my word on that.'

'As you appear to have made up your mind, I will save my breath,' said Grizelda with deep displeasure.

'But at least you will admit that a railway gives you a far speedier and more convenient way of travelling. When you leave Fetherstone for London I'll be bound you take the train from Bending Junction, if you do insist upon travelling in your own coach mounted on one of its trucks. And is it not better to travel in such a way, reaching London in an hour and a half, than taking six to seven hours in the old travelling coach, having to break your journey every ten miles or so for the horses to be baited? Railway travel is the only locomotion for the future, Grizel, and it will not be long before you put your pride in your pocket and travel as the rest of us are doing in a comfortable first-class railway carriage.'

'Sitting opposite strangers in the same carriage!' she exclaimed. 'Never! It would be most improper.'

He continued imperturbably: 'At all events those critics who declared ten years ago or more that the railways would be the end of the horse in Britain have been as confounded there as in all the other things they said. Our cities have *not* been filled with vile-smelling smoke, our charming villages have *not* been turned into dirty great towns – with the exception of little Swindon, of course! – and the cattle in the fields have *not* been suffocated. But if you persuade Oliver to refuse to have the Bending–Worcester railway through his land Sir Giles Spender will be delighted to make money out of his ruined acres. Both estates have been surveyed and it is for Oliver himself to decide.'

'The Fetherstone acres are not ruined,' said her ladyship obstinately. 'And that is why they must be saved from this wretched railway company. I am determined over this, Julian, raise your eyebrows as you will. I will not allow it, whatever Oliver says to the contrary.'

He got up from the winged armchair where he had been sitting: he was a tall man and Lady Fetherstone was a small woman, and though her eyes were sparkling with defiance his height gave him the advantage over her.

'Grizel, my dear,' he said gravely, 'have a care of what you are doing. I warn you, Oliver is becoming tired of petticoat government, and you will not be able to dictate to him much longer. He has set his heart on this scheme and if you do anything to thwart him he will not forgive you. I would remind you that your eldest son has inherited your own determination under his boyish ways, and it will serve him far better than his father's sleepy inactivity. But I have said my say and I can see I have wasted my time. Is Oliver with you?'

'He is in the park this morning trying out a new carriage.'

'Then perhaps you will be kind enough to ask him to call on me at my house in Bedford Square tomorrow morning at ten o'clock? I am anxious to have him with me when I visit the offices of the railway company at Euston.'

'I will give him your message and I daresay he will be there.' She added after a moment, 'You ought to stand for Parliament, Julian. Once Oliver is of age you will have nothing to do.'

'Not me. You are in London for the season, I take it?'

'Until the end of June, when we shall return to Fetherstone for the coming-of-age celebrations in July.'

Her more gracious manner did not soften him. He said goodbye stiffly and as he walked back to his bachelor establishment in Bedford Square he thought ironically of the house he had just left. The builder Cubitt had built it to the late Lord Fetherstone's design, and he wondered if, when she surveyed the square of elegant houses outside her windows, Grizelda remembered that only twenty years earlier it had been a rough piece of ground used by troopers of the Household Cavalry for exercising their horses in the daytime, and much frequented by footpads at night. She might have felt that here was an occasion when progress could be said to be a good thing, although there had been considerable opposition to the plan at the time as ruining the rural aspect of the district and spreading the town into the countryside.

He reflected that as far as he was concerned his ward's

coming of age could not be soon enough. Oliver's father had been an excellent husband and father, he had stood for Parliament and had been respectfully listened to when he got there, but his one besetting sin had been procrastination. He hated to make decisions, and no doubt he would have put off the prospective railway line had he been alive now. But since his death his widow had appeared to regard Julian as her property: he was there not only as Oliver's guardian but to manage everything for her too in the way of business, until he despaired of persuading her that there were others more qualified than he was. Their lawyer in Lincoln's Inn for example, had a far better knowledge of the family's finances, and the agent Duffy was at Fetherstone to advise on the house and the estate. But even her eldest daughter's marriage had to be planned with Julian's approval, although her ladyship never took his advice when it conflicted with her own inclinations. Letters pursued him nearly every day of the week, and when the two younger girls Augusta and Sarah had come out during the year following their sister's wedding he had to be consulted on the ball that was to be given in Eaton Square and the guests who were to be asked or left out, simply, he thought, to be told that he was wrong in nearly every instance.

He was beginning to find it extremely tiresome, and he swore that after July he would have no more of it. Her ladyship could go to her son, his agent or his man of business to advise her, and quarrel with them instead of with him. In fact in his more maddened moments he said he would give up his London house and seek one in the Outer Hebrides.

'How you do bully that poor man, Mamma!' Augusta said after he had gone.

'I do not bully him at all,' said Grizelda. 'But like all

57

men he is very obstinate over things that do not affect him.'

'Mamma.' Sarah was tired of the railway and checked a fresh outburst with a swift change of subject. 'Isn't it today that Susanna's new governess arrives?'

'I believe she is coming this week.' Her mamma was surprised at the question. 'Why do you ask, my dear?'

'Because,' said Sarah slowly, 'I would like to have been there to welcome her.'

'Welcome a *governess*? What can you mean?' Grizelda laughed. 'Mrs Glynn is there, my love. There is no fear that she will not see that Miss Lakesby has all she needs.'

'There!' said Sarah. 'Lakesby! That is what I meant when I said I would have liked to be there to welcome her – to see if she is a relation of the girl who was Charlotte Tremayne's friend when we were staying at Mayne four years ago. It was before Phemie's wedding and Sylvia Tremayne was to be a bridesmaid. Don't you remember Charlotte's friend, Mamma – a schoolgirl of the same age as Charlotte with the most lovely auburn hair? She had a pretty name too – Allegra. I would have liked to ask our Miss Lakesby if she is a relative of Allegra's and where she is now.'

'Well, you will have time to ask her all the questions you like in June,' said her mamma. 'And I daresay she will answer them if she can. Her name is Agnes I believe, and I daresay she may be a distant relative of the family. But very distant, or she would scarcely be earning her bread as a governess would she?'

Sarah agreed. 'I wonder if she is as pretty as Allegra?' she said.

'I hope not!' Lady Fetherstone was alarmed. 'You know how susceptible Oliver is, and he is often at Fetherstone when we are in London. I would not like to have a pretty governess for him to flirt with there.'

'I believe you would keep Oliver in a glass case if you could, Mamma,' said Augusta mischievously.

'You must admit, my dear, that your eldest brother falls in and out of love very easily.' Grizelda laughed, however, if somewhat reluctantly. 'There is safety in numbers, I suppose.'

Oliver's latest inamorata had been the daughter of a learned gentleman at Oxford: she had been several years older than he, and her ladyship had descended upon Oxford without delay to persuade the girl that it was only a case of calf-love and no more. Shortly afterwards she had married a schoolmaster, releasing Oliver from his vows of everlasting love, and he had sulked for quite some time. Her ladyship still congratulated herself on her triumphant conclusion of the affair.

'He is not likely,' she told her daughters complacently, 'to fall seriously in love with a governess!'

6

Julian Armitage's message was passed on to Lord
Fetherstone who arrived in Bedford Square punctually
at ten o'clock on the following morning in his new
carriage. His guardian looked at it with disgust.

'You can send that back to Eaton Square,' he said
shortly. 'I am not going to have it entangled in the
wheels of every hackney cab in London on the way to
Euston. We will walk, my boy. It will do you good.'

So the carriage was sent back and they set out together on foot. Oliver had been staying with his mother's
father, a choleric old gentleman with an earldom and
vast estates in Cheshire, and when Julian asked if he
had heard much about the Bending–Worcester railway
while he was there he replied lightly that her letters of
protest had descended upon him like leaves in an
autumn gale.

'Is the Earl in favour of it?'

'Need you ask, sir? He lives in the North Country
where railways are become as natural as the air one
breathes. He says I'd be a fool to refuse the Company's
offer, and that Mamma, being a female, does not understand such matters. She appears to have a rigid dislike
for railways, but I daresay she will come round in time.'

Julian did not feel quite so sure. 'I think we should
study the plan in more detail before we sign any papers,
and discover if the track will be as offensive as your
mamma fears.' He enquired how Oliver intended to
employ his time on the estates at Fetherstone and in
Yorkshire.

'I shall consult my agents and ride round the properties whenever I am there,' Oliver said carelessly. 'Getting to know my tenants and all that. I prefer Fetherstone to Yorkshire – the house there is a barracks of a place and not to my liking at all, though it is supposed to be very great. I shall spend most of my time at Fetherstone, which I intend to improve – not the house,' he added hastily, as Mr Armitage's face exhibited some apprehension, 'but the village. It needs a number of improvements, and I would like to introduce gas-lighting there. If I cannot find that the Bending Gas Company is willing to extend its supplies to Fetherstone I daresay I shall have a gasometer built into the grounds. I know the exact spot I shall select for it, in the shrubberies near the west wing. It would be an excellent thing to have the principal rooms and corridors illuminated by gas.'

'Have you mentioned this to your mamma?'

'Good God, no. The railway is enough for her to swallow at one time. I shall not consider it seriously before the end of the summer, when I am my own master, and I promise you, sir, that you shall not be dragged into any such discussions once I am of age. You will be free of my estates and problems.'

His determination was encouraging: Mr Armitage thanked him and his mind turned less longingly towards the Outer Hebrides.

The offices of the Bending Junction–Worcester Railway Company were small and dark with no pretensions to grandeur: the company was, after all, only a branch line on the London–Birmingham Railway and except for its situation it might have been the offices of some down-at-heel stock jobber. The furniture was scanty, a solitary ink-stained deal table strewn with papers and two chairs, one being occupied by Mr Beauchamp, the Company's secretary. A picture of George Stephenson's Rocket adorned the wall over the fireplace, in which a small fire burned sulkily, and the wall opposite the grimy window was adorned with a large map.

What made the room look even smaller was the broad-shouldered man standing with his back to the fire, a light-coloured tall hat on the back of his head, his coat-tails thrown over his wrists and his hands thrust deep in his trousers pockets. His hair was black as was the fringe of whiskers round his chin, and his eyes under their bushy brows were the brilliant blue of the Celts. He was not introduced to Lord Fetherstone or his guardian, and they thought at first that he was some underling who had come to the secretary for directions.

Mr Beauchamp was in his late fifties with a thin face and an attenuated figure, as if he snatched meals when he could and suffered in consequence from dyspepsia. He received the gentlemen with deference, while his companion went into the outer office to summon a clerk and tell him to fetch another chair.

'That, gentlemen, is the Company's engineer, Mr William Buckhurst,' Mr Beauchamp told them. 'He has only recently arrived back in England: he has gained a fine reputation for his work on railroads and was talking of retirement when our contractor persuaded him to work on the Bending–Worcester line. His fee is not a small one, but at least we know that in his hands it will go forward with efficiency and speed and without too great a price in lives.'

He caught Mr Armitage's startled look and explained smiling: 'There is bound to be some loss of life in building a railway, the workmen will take unnecessary risks when wheeling loaded trucks and barrows, and indulge in horse-play and things of that sort. Mr Buckhurst did a preliminary survey of the Fetherstone land at the same time as he did one of the Spender property, Sir Giles being very anxious that it should go his way, but Mr Buckhurst says this would lengthen the track by at least ten miles, and at a cost of four thousand pounds a mile it would be a serious consideration, although against that we must balance the cost of building a short bridge over the River Fether.'

As his visitors made no comment he continued, 'I am empowered to say that the Company is prepared to pay handsomely for the land, in fact they are offering three times the normal value per acre.' He added as an afterthought, 'I might perhaps mention that one or two gentlemen through whose estates the line will run have asked if they might have small private stations erected to accommodate their families and their guests.'

'That's a corking good notion,' said his lordship, whose attention until then had been concentrated on the Rocket. 'I daresay I might have one built at Fetherstone when the railway reaches it.' He caught Mr Armitage's warning glance and went on engagingly: 'My mamma imagines that your railroad will spoil the view from the house, which is why Mr Armitage and I are here today, to study your plans in more detail so that we may dispell such fears.'

'The plan is behind you on that wall, my lord.' Mr Buckhurst had returned with a clerk carrying two chairs, and he joined them in front of the map where the Fetherstone line was outlined in red and the Spender route in blue. With the aid of his pocket knife he showed exactly where the line would enter the valley below the Copley hills.

'It enters at Copley's Gate,' he explained in his pleasant country-bred voice, 'then it crosses the meadows on the far side of the meadows below the beechwoods.'

'At a safe distance, I trust?' put in Mr Armitage. 'In warm weather the hot ashes from your engines could set the whole of those woods alight, and beechwood is valuable.'

'I guarantee that it will be at a safe distance, sir.'

'You cannot build it nearer the river?'

'No, sir. The ground there is marshy and it would mean raising the railroad on piles driven into the mud. It would be a difficult and hazardous undertaking.'

'It would also be more visible from the house, which would not please my mamma,' put in Oliver. 'Where is the river bridge to come?'

'On the east side of the Horseshoe, my lord, out of sight of the house altogether. After that it will traverse four miles of your lordship's property before leaving it, but none of that will be seen from the house either.'

'But it will take some of my best farmland,' said his lordship shrewdly, surprising Mr Armitage. 'I conclude the Company will be prepared to compensate my farmers handsomely for the excellent land they will be required to forfeit?'

Mr Buckhurst, echoed by Mr Beauchamp, was able to reassure him on this point, and then Mr Armitage raised another problem with the secretary. 'We have all heard that wherever they make their railroads the gangs of navvies leave a trail of destruction behind them, and small and pretty villages like Fetherstone have been completely ruined, the navvies' huts and tents transforming them into large sprawling slums, which often remain a permanent eyesore. I would like Mr Buckhurst's assurance, before his lordship puts his hand to anything, that his contractor does not intend to use Fetherstone village as a lodgement for his gangs?'

'There will be nothing of that sort there.' Buckhurst was decided about that. 'I have already discussed it with him, and we have agreed that it is too small a village for such a purpose. Our workmen will be lodged first in Bending, until they enter the Fetherstone property, when their headquarters will be transferred to Sprackley, which is unlikely to be spoiled by such an invasion.' Sprackley was a large and ugly town with several thriving manufactories by which the coming of the branch line would be welcomed. 'Twenty thousand men – which is the number estimated we shall need for this line – will not make an appreciable disruption there. They will be encamped round the town.'

Mr Armitage remembered Bending before it became Bending Junction with some nostalgia. Until the London–Birmingham railway reached it, it had been a pleasant little market town, but after the gangs arrived with their trucks and their barrows and their pickaxes it had looked as if an earthquake had struck.

'I suggest that Lord Fetherstone and I pay one last visit to Castle Fetherstone before we conclude the matter,' he said. 'We will ride over the full extent of the track with his lordship's agent within the next few days, and if we think there should be any alteration made to the plan we will inform you, Mr Beauchamp, immediately.'

William Buckhurst produced a copy of the plan for their agent to study and Mr Beauchamp said he would look forward to hearing from his lordship at an early date.

'We hope to have this plan included in the list that is to go before Parliament next session,' he said. 'And if it is passed our contractor can gather his gangs together and the thing should be complete in the space of – two years, did you say, William?'

'Possibly less,' said Mr Buckhurst. 'The plan is for a single track with slipways and I reckon two years should be sufficient – unless Mr Hudson decides to take a hand in it, when anything might happen to throw us off course.'

' "King" Hudson?' said Oliver smiling.

'Yes, my lord, "King" Hudson,' said Mr Buckhurst grimly, as Mr Beauchamp saw them to the door. After they had gone Mr Buckhurst asked if Lord Fetherstone proposed to buy any shares in the Company.

'On the contrary, if the thing goes through it is the Company who will be paying his lordship.'

'Excellent. I would rather his lordship were paid for his land than put his money into a railway that may not exist should Hudson hear of it. He has a habit of devouring small companies for his breakfast.'

'You're a cynical old devil, ain't you?' Mr Beauchamp lighted a cigar.

'I have returned to England to find "King" Hudson very much in my way,' complained Mr Buckhurst. 'He travels round the country with that abominable circus of sycophants, and he is making far too much money for himself. When the day of reckoning comes God help the small investor, because nobody else will.' He settled his hat on his head with a thump of his fist on its crown and turned towards the door. 'I will collect my young surveyors the moment you tell me that the Fetherstone acres are yours.'

There was a train on the point of leaving for Paragay and after a moment's hesitation Mr Buckhurst thought he would take it. If the railway he was to work on became a fact then it would be to his interest to live near enough to make frequent visits to the track when it was in progress. When it was finished he determined to adhere to his decision to give up further projects, being in no mind to work himself to death over railway ventures for others to enjoy. He intended to buy a small country property where he could settle down with a wife and raise a family.

His parents were dead, he had no near relatives left, and although his ideas were nebulous, he knew that the house he wanted must be comfortable but not over large, with a pleasant garden, an orchard, and a paddock for a few horses. Of the lady who would be its mistress he had but a hazy idea: his work had not left him much time for mixing with the opposite sex. But it must be admitted that since he had taken that journey from Paragay to Bending Junction with Miss Lakesby his thoughts had tended to dwell on ladies with hair of a rich auburn tint.

As he mounted to a first-class compartment that morning he was surprised and pleased to find Jack Willoughby seated there.

'This is an unexpected pleasure,' he said. 'You are travelling, I take it, to see your mother?'

'To Paragay,' smiled Willoughby, moving his valise from the opposite seat so that Buckhurst could sit there. 'I suppose you are for Bending Junction?'

'Not until the final route has been settled.' He added that it was the last railway he intended to have anything to do with. 'That is why I am going to Paragay this morning, to look for a property where I can settle down, and it happens to be the sort of small country town that would suit me admirably. I have neither the money nor the inclination to live in a large country place: your country squires frighten me. They are too high and mighty for the son of a village wheelwright. But in a town like Paragay society is mixed and kinder to strangers. I think I could settle there very well.'

'You are fortunate to be able to think of retirement,' said Willoughby enviously. 'You're a clever devil, Buckhurst, and I am doubtful if you will be allowed to be idle so early in life. I hear you spoken of everywhere, while I am still only put to design small branch lines that often come to nothing.'

'I served a hard apprenticeship,' Buckhurst reminded him.

'That is so.' The other glanced at him keenly. 'Do you plan to marry?'

'If I can find a lady ready and willing to take me for what I am,' said Mr Buckhurst equably.

'With your fortune they'll be willing and ready enough, my dear fellow,' said Jack Willoughby, smiling, and Buckhurst changed the subject rather quickly to his son, Midshipman Willoughby. How was he progressing in the Navy, did he like his captain, and what did the future hold for the boy? From there they returned to Paragay and Mrs Willoughby's liking for the town, and presently Mr Buckhurst casually introduced the name of Lakesby. Did Mr Willoughby know the family well?

'No, but my mother knows them all. Mrs Henry Lakesby has not long been a resident of Well Walk. Mamma feels sorry for Mr Eustace Lakesby, who inherited an estate crippled with debts. Henry Lakesby, though a charming man, was quite irresponsible where providing for his wife and daughter was concerned.' He chuckled suddenly. 'I hear that Miss Allegra has gone out to be a governess, no doubt to scandalize her relations and friends. Mamma dismisses it as being an escapade — the result of a high-spirited girl being suddenly confined to the society of a small town. Her mamma and her aunt are very ready to make friends with all their neighbours, but Allegra puts her head in the air and refuses to know them. But that is only what one might expect from a girl with red hair.'

'Auburn,' corrected Mr Buckhurst, but the noise of the train drowned his voice.

'And a temper,' continued Mr Willoughby. 'Ready to flare up over nothing.'

Mr Buckhurst said that he had met her once when he was asked by her cousin Robert to accompany her to Bending Junction. 'She was on her way to her situation then I believe.'

'I daresay she was, and it was like Robert to put her

68

in the charge of a stranger. I daresay she was very off-hand with you?'

'On the contrary, we had an interesting conversation,' said Mr Buckhurst, but could not suppress a slight embarrassment in his manner and Willoughby laughed.

'I see she made an impression on you,' he observed. 'But it is no use looking for a wife in that quarter, my friend. She has refused several offers, it is said, and a railway engineer will scarcely appeal to Miss Allegra Lakesby, however much money he may have made. Her family goes back to the Conquest, so I have been told.'

'I daresay mine does too,' said Mr Buckhurst, quite unruffled by his friend's teasing. 'I would like to help the family if it were possible. She mentioned some land of her mother's near Beccles. Is there any hope of a railway in that direction? The land appears to be of little value, but if a company wanted it sufficiently I daresay they would pay a few hundreds for it.'

'A railway was planned for that part of the coast but has recently been abandoned,' Willoughby told him. 'I happen to know about it because I had to draft the initial plan. I am not working for the Eastern Counties Company now, but had Mrs Lakesby's land been near Burston it might have been a very different matter. There is a railroad planned from Burston through Haughley to Norwich in the near future – the plans have been got out so I am told, and it is hoped to submit them to Parliament this coming session. But Burston is many miles from Beccles.'

Mr Buckhurst agreed and dismissed Mrs Lakesby's barren inheritance from his mind, asking about the work Willoughby was engaged on – a branch line in Somerset – and their conversation became purely technical until the train arrived at Paragay.

There, just as they were parting, Mr Willoughby said

that if Mr Buckhurst were serious in wishing to purchase a small property in Paragay he might do worse than the Grange on the western outskirts of the town. 'I believe it may be up for sale shortly – the owner, Colonel Woodley, died in January and it is said that Mrs Woodley wishes to exchange it for a smaller house in Bath where she has relatives.'

Mr Buckhurst said that he would remember it and with a warm handshake they parted.

7

On the night of their arrival at Castle Fetherstone, after they had dined, young Lord Fetherstone and his guardian put their heads together over Mr Buckhurst's plan looking for objections but finding none, and the next morning early they were up and riding with Mr Duffy along the route. They entered it by Copley's Gate and followed it to where the bridge was planned, crossing the river further up by a shallow ford. On the way, before the east shoulder of the Horseshoe hid it from sight they paused a while to look across the valley at the mansion on the southern slopes, and found that it was dwarfed by the distance between it and the proposed route through the valley. They came to the conclusion that any question of intrusion on its privacy was sheer nonsense and continued along the track without finding any more serious objection than the disappearance of several acres of good farmland.

Mr Armitage returned to London on the following day satisfied that he had done all he could to calm Grizelda's fears for her view and her privacy, and armed with Oliver's request that he would close with the Company's offer at once.

Oliver stayed on at Fetherstone to examine the plan in more detail, and spent some hours with Mr Duffy discussing the possibility of planting more trees between the proposed line and the river.

Then he went from room to room in the house with Mrs Glynn, making a note of those that looked towards the beechwoods where smoke might be seen on a very clear day, following this with a stroll in those parts of the grounds where it also might be visible. Occupied in this way on that afternoon he heard voices and laughter coming from the direction of the old bowling green to the east of the house. Years previously his father had set this apart for his children's playground, the roots from the surrounding trees making the ground too uneven for the game for which it was planned. He remembered that he had not paid his usual visit to Susanna in the schoolroom since he had arrived and he strolled across the terraced lawns to the iron gate set in the wall that surrounded the bowling green and pushed it open.

The four Spender children, aged from six to eleven, were there, playing ball with his sister. A girl in a brown dress and a plain straw bonnet was playing with them, entering into the game as if she were an elder sister, while Miss Troy, the Spenders' governess, sat on a bench watching them, thankful to rest her feet.

Oliver stood there for several minutes watching the girl, whose graceful movements enchanted him, and then Susanna saw him and raced to him to be caught up and kissed.

The girl in the brown dress turned her head and saw him and the laughter died out of her face. She walked off sedately to join Miss Troy, who said that she thought it was time they went indoors for the children's tea. The March afternoon was becoming cold and Nurse Capper would be wondering what had become of them.

Oliver, however, did not intend to allow the young woman to escape him so easily.

'Who is that?' he asked Susanna.

'Miss Lakesby, my new governess, and I love her,' said Susanna happily.

Oliver crossed the lawn to say good-day to Miss Troy and to be introduced to Miss Lakesby, and the shock of hearing that she was the governess did not prevent him from seeing that she was one of the prettiest girls he had ever met.

'I think,' he said briskly, 'I will come and have a schoolroom tea with you, Susanna. It is a treat I have been denied for too long.'

The children were delighted and conducted him into the house by the east door and up the east staircase that led imposingly to the upper floors and the schoolroom. Miss Troy and Allegra followed, burdened with coats and hats that had been thrown off, and refusing Oliver's offers to relieve them of their burdens, Allegra especially very correct with 'my lord' and 'your lordship'. As they were going upstairs, Miss Troy whispered to her that it was the first time his lordship had ever offered to carry anything for her, or indeed had even summoned a footman to do it. 'It must be your pretty face that has made him so gallant, my dear,' she said with a smile that was more amused than resentful.

It was a remark that Allegra remembered that evening as she went to change her dress for her early supper in the schoolroom. She happened to see one of the doors on her corridor open and a maid was hanging a curtain in a small bedroom there.

She had noticed as she had passed down the corridor from time to time that the doors had labels on them, and as she looked closer at the one that was open she saw a bell hanging inside. The label on the door was the Honourable Augusta, and the one next to it had the title, the Honourable Sarah, but she could not think that members of the family slept there. She stopped to ask the girl who used the room in which she was hanging the curtains.

'This is Miss Dinstan's room – Miss Augusta's maid,' said the girl, turning from her task to smile at her. 'And the one next to it is Miss Fuller's room – she's Miss Sarah's maid. All the rooms on this corridor is for ladies' maids, miss.'

Allegra thanked her and went on to her room, considering her own status in the household. It seemed that she was a little above the ordinary run of the servants and on a level with the ladies' maids, in which case it was possible that Mr Buckhurst had been right in suggesting that she could find herself on the wrong side of the door.

This idea was emphasized later when she was finishing her supper and Oliver sent an invitation to the schoolroom for her to dine with him that night.

The young man was all she had dreamed of in her flights of romance, but his manner in the schoolroom had a familiarity that had surprised and annoyed her. This invitation sent by a footman increased that annoyance, and she sent back a message by the man in a tone that took the cheeky grin off his face, that Miss Lakesby sent her compliments and thanks to his lordship but she had already dined.

The news of the invitation leaked out, however, and the next evening on her visit to the housekeeper's parlour Mrs Capper commented on it to her friend Mrs Glynn. 'What did I tell you, ma'am?' she said ominously. 'She is far too pretty to be a governess.'

Mrs Glynn agreed. 'Not but what she didn't act very properly,' she added, 'and put his lordship in his place, which is how it should be. She is too much of a lady to do otherwise, Mrs Capper, and I wouldn't be surprised if she's as well born as his lordship, if truth were known. But I'm afraid her ladyship will send her packing if he gets up to many of these capers, and I shall be sorry if 'tis so, because she's one of the nicest young ladies I've ever known. For a governess, that is to say.'

It was evident that Mrs Glynn had no doubt whatever as to which side of the door a governess belonged.

Oliver knew perfectly well that a flirtation with Miss Lakesby would be frowned upon by his mamma even more than his liking for the new railroad, and smarting

74

under an unaccustomed snub he found himself thinking about the governess more than he liked. It was very seldom that a young woman in such an inferior position could withstand being noticed by young Lord Fetherstone.

Moreover, his youngest sister, having discovered him to be there, found him out and followed him whenever her lessons permitted, and as she had been engaged for the purpose her governess was forced to accompany her. Oliver found therefore that he had plenty of occasions in which to study Miss Lakesby at his leisure.

Not that she repaid him for his studies: in matters of dress she had the taste of a superior servant, while her expression continued to be grave and prim whenever they met. But neither its gravity nor its primness could hide the beauty of her face.

'So,' he said, meeting them on his way to the stables one morning as they were starting out for their morning walk, 'that old fool Scrimmy has left at last. Something to do with an ailing father I believe. I hope you have not an ailing father to call you home, Miss Lakesby?' His eyes might be admiring but she detected the odious familiarity in his manner again and it offended her almost beyond endurance.

'My father is dead,' she said shortly. 'And your lordship is wrong in thinking Miss Scrimger to be a fool. I am very pleased with the way Miss Susanna has been taught. Her handwriting needs some correction but she is doing her best to improve it.' The governess attitude might be overdone, but it snubbed him as neatly as one of his sisters' friends might have done had he used the same tone with her. He felt his temper slipping a little: he wished she would not keep saying 'your lordship' and he said, wanting to see her colour, 'You are young to be a governess.'

'That is a fault I hope to grow out of, my lord.' There

was no mistaking the edge to her voice. 'And now if your lordship will excuse me I must attend to my charge.' And she hurried to Susanna, who had raced on ahead and fallen and grazed her knees and was threatening to bawl her head off.

'Damn you and your lordships,' said Oliver, as he went on to the stables in a huff, to spend the rest of the day visiting tenants, discussing business affairs with Mr Duffy, and trying to forget a young woman who threatened to interest him even more than the handsome Julia who had been sent packing by his formidable mamma.

He did not give in easily and the following morning a polite little note was sent to the schoolroom asking if Miss Lakesby would bring Susanna to take luncheon with her brother that day.

In some perplexity and feeling that here was a situation where she needed advice, Allegra took the note to Mrs Capper and asked what she should do. 'Does her ladyship have Miss Susanna down to luncheon when she is here?' she asked.

'Sometimes when she is alone.' The old nurse considered the matter carefully. 'As Miss Susanna is to go to take tea with Lady Spender's children today,' she said then, 'and it is a drive of eight miles to Manning Place I think it would be wise for her to have a quiet luncheon with you in the schoolroom, Miss Lakesby.' She saw the relief in the girl's face and added that Miss Susanna was easily excited.

'So she is.' Allegra hesitated. 'Shall I write to his lordship and tell him so – or will you see him for me, Mrs Capper?'

The old woman was touched by the appeal in the dark eyes. 'The poor young thing spoke like as if I were her nurse as well as Miss Susanna's!' she told Mrs Glynn later.

'You leave his lordship to me, my dear,' she said, and she sailed off downstairs like a female Iron Duke.

Oliver knew when he was beaten and he did not care to pursue so ungrateful a young woman any longer. The next day he left for Eaton Square, where he was warmly welcomed. His mother's sister, Lady Maria Huckley, was staying there on her way to a wedding in Shropshire, with her two daughters, Miriam and Elizabeth, and Oliver sang duets with Miriam after dinner and flirted with Elizabeth and found it very comforting to his ego. Later on when his mamma asked if he had seen Susanna's new governess he replied with a carelessness that did not deceive her for a moment that he believed he did. He thought he had noticed that old Scrimmy had been replaced by someone else.

'Miss Lakesby, the governess who has taken Miss Scrimger's place, is very young,' Grizelda observed. 'Is she a good-looking girl, Oliver?'

'I am afraid I did not pay her sufficient attention to notice,' he replied, but there was a flicker in his eyes that reminded her of his father when he had not been speaking the truth. 'Had I known that you wished for a report on her appearance, Mamma, I would have been more particular.' And he turned the conversation swiftly to the impending railroad at Fetherstone and succeeded in taking her mind off Susanna and her new governess.

'If you give your consent to that railroad, Oliver,' she told him severely, 'it will be enough to make your father turn in his grave.'

'My dearest Mamma, my revered parent was far too lethargic by nature in his lifetime to become a spinning top in his grave.' He added that he intended to invite some of his Oxford friends to Fetherstone to help him shoot the crows that were being a nuisance to his gamekeepers.

'Invite whom you like, my love,' said Lady Fetherstone. 'But impress on them to bring their own guns. Some of those in the gun-room are too old to be safe.'

Her fears were lulled for a moment, but when she went upstairs with her sister that night to have their usual little private chat before she went to bed she told her that she was far from satisfied and that she thought there was Something Going On. When pressed to explain, she said that Mrs Glynn had referred to Miss Lakesby as being a pretty young lady, which was not as she usually described a governess. 'I have no doubt that she belongs to a poor branch of the Lakesby family,' she added, 'but if she has their looks – and some of them were a handsome lot – you know what Oliver is like over pretty girls. He was far too evasive over his replies to my enquiries about her, but as I cannot leave London until the end of June I do not see what I can do.'

Her sister suggested that she and her daughters should visit Castle Fetherstone on their way to Shropshire. 'It will not be very much out of our way. I will act as Oliver's hostess when his friends are visiting him and the girls will help to entertain them, and he could perhaps invite others of your friends in the neighbourhood to a few evening parties while we are there, if you have no objection, Grizel.'

Lady Fetherstone had no objection in the world. 'You will then be able to observe this new governess and judge of her behaviour for me,' she said.

'And I will write to you before I leave Fetherstone and tell you what I think of her,' added her sister.

So it was arranged. Oliver wrote to half a dozen of his friends, asking them to direct their replies to Fetherstone and to arrive with their guns by the following Friday. His aunt and cousins promised to arrive on the same day, and he tried to keep his mind from dwelling on Miss Lakesby. He wished that her eyes had not been so scornful the last time they had met and he determined to break through the reserve that encompassed her like a prickly hedge.

He returned to Castle Fetherstone the following Wednesday and found replies from his friends waiting for him, promising their guns, their powder-horns, and their dogs to help dispose of the troublesome crows.

8

Oliver's father had designed a cottage orné at one end
of the bowling green for the enjoyment of his family.
It was built in the shade of a large tulip tree, and it
was, he told them, to be their own house: the children
were its owners and they would take turns to play host
and hostess to their parents and their friends when they
received them there as their guests.

Inside the cottage there was a parlour, with a copper
kettle on the hob beside its hearth, while a tiny kitchen
held china bowls for mixing flour for cakes, and even
an oven in the centre chimney in which they could be
baked.

When they were children Oliver and his sisters and
younger brothers had delighted in the little house, but
as they grew older there had only been an occasional
picnic tea there, brought in baskets from the house with
cakes from the still-room. The little parlour was gradually used for the storing of cricket bats and bows and
arrows and a target stuffed with straw, and gardening
tools that they used for their gardens that surrounded
the green.

Now that Euphemia was married and Augusta and
Sarah were out and the younger boys at Eton College
and too superior by half for such infantile employment,
the cottage was kept for Susanna's amusement alone
when she had her small friends to tea.

Having read his letters that Wednesday and feeling
in a more amiable mood, Oliver took a stroll with his
old dog Rufus in the afternoon, and as he returned to
the south front by way of one of the lower terraces he

caught sight of a curl of smoke issuing from where the cottage was situated.

He pushed open the iron gate and saw that the smoke was coming from the cottage chimney and he crossed the lawn and went in, to find the Spender children gathered round the table with Susanna, eating bread and honey and slices of plum cake. At the head of the table behind a large teapot sat Miss Troy, while at the foot Allegra was trying to prevent the honey from the children's hands being spread over their clothes. In the kitchen Mrs Capper was in charge of the commissariat.

The children welcomed him with enthusiasm and a chair was sought for him to join them at the table, but when it was clear that every chair in the cottage was in use Allegra quickly vacated hers, saying that Mrs Capper required her assistance in the kitchen. 'She is badly in need of a kitchen-maid,' she told Miss Troy, smiling, and left her to pour out tea for his lordship at whom she had not looked at all.

He was forced to stay and listen to the vapourings of the Spenders' lady and after tea he suggested a game of cricket, hoping that Miss Lakesby would join them, but she remained out of sight in the kitchen, and he soon handed the bat to Thomas Spender and left the bowling green with Rufus. He glanced at the cottage windows under the branches of the tulip tree as he passed and saw Miss Lakesby standing there with her sleeves rolled up, busy washing up cups and saucers and plates in a bowl of hot water at the kitchen table there, while Nurse Capper wiped them and restored them to their cupboard. As she worked she talked and laughed with the old woman and he went his way angrily, telling himself that she was an ungrateful little hussy and he would think of her no more.

That evening, however, as Mrs Capper was folding Susanna's clothes ready for the morning she looked for the child's thick mantle that had been taken to the cottage in case she was not warm enough in a thinner one.

'You should have brought it back with you, Miss Lakesby,' grumbled the old nurse. 'If the wind should change – and warm as it was today we are still only in March – if I had to put her into the thin mantle tomorrow because the thicker one could not be found she might catch her death. It doesn't matter how warm the day is "ne'er cast a clout till May is out".'

Allegra apologized and said she would run down to the cottage and fetch it.

'Nay, I'll send one of the servants for it,' said the old woman, somewhat mollified. Most governesses would have taken offence at her sharpness.

'No, I will go. It is bright moonlight outside and I shall see my way clearly.' Allegra fetched a shawl from her room and ran down the narrow stairs from the ladies' maids' corridor to the door in the east wing. It was only a few minutes from there to the little wicket gate in the north side of the bowling green, and as she reached the cottage the moon threw a silvery light over it, falling in pools of light through the latticed windows. She found the mantle easily and was about to return with it when a shadow separated itself swiftly from the tulip tree and filled the cottage doorway. She stopped short, startled, and Oliver came into the little parlour, shutting and locking the door behind him and slipping the key into his pocket.

'Lord Fetherstone!' She was indignant and angry. 'Kindly unlock that door and remove yourself from the doorway.'

'Not until I'm paid for it,' he said smiling. 'It is no good putting on airs with me, my dear. You are only the governess here – not a fine lady. I want a kiss before the key comes out of my pocket.'

'On the contrary, you will do as I say.' She retreated quickly, putting the table between them, her voice taking the tone that she would have used to a disrespectful servant at the Manor. 'Unlock that door and go and stand by the fireplace and do not move until I have gone. Do you understand me?'

'I understand you, my dear. Parsons' daughters are brought up to be prim and proper, but you are not in your father's parsonage now and what is a kiss? Come, pay up!'

He took a step towards her and she did not move from behind the table: it was a very solid one. 'I am not a parson's daughter,' she said. 'And if I were it does not give you leave to behave as no gentleman should to a person in his mother's employment. You will unlock that door, Lord Fetherstone, and you will let me go without molesting me in any way, because if you do not the moment I reach my room tonight I shall send a servant for my portmanteau and I shall pack and leave tomorrow, and when I arrive home I shall write to Lady Fetherstone explaining the reason for my behaviour.'

'You do not mean that!' He laughed a shade uneasily.

'I mean every word of it.' Her chin lifted. 'Unlock that door at once, if you please.'

'Oh very well, if you intend to make an issue of it. He unlocked the door and threw it open.

'Now go and stand by the fireplace.' As he hesitated, her voice sharpened. 'At once, my lord!'

He crossed to the fireplace and she walked out with the air of a duchess. He stayed in the cottage for a few minutes, angry and slightly ashamed, but chiefly puzzled. If it were not for the girl's position in the household he would have said that she came from the same class as himself. There was an air of command about her, a fine dignity and an anger entirely different from the airs one would expect from a pretty governess.

He wondered who she was: Lakesby was a good name but he thought it likely that she had no legal claim to it.

As for Allegra she hardly knew how she got back with Susanna's mantle. In that short interview with the young man all her romantic dreams had been shattered. Heroes, it seemed, came in all guises, but it appeared that perhaps tall and handsome ones did not put young ladies on pedestals or treat them like bits of porcelain.

'Are you feeling well, dear?' Nurse Capper glanced at her anxiously as she took Susanna's mantle from her. 'You are looking very white.'

'The cottage looked quite ghostly in the moonlight.' Allegra turned it off with a laugh. 'A shadow moved and for a moment I was frightened.'

'I should have sent a servant,' said Mrs Capper, and made her some hot chocolate before she went to bed.

The next day Oliver spent riding with Duffy and promising his tenants that their problems would be solved with the coming of the railway. He did not go near the bowling green and when he saw Susanna out with her governess he submitted to her greeting with brotherly affection and rewarded her governess with a stiff unsmiling good-day which she ignored.

March, having come in like a lion, was going out like a lamb, and a few days of warm weather anticipated April. The day before Oliver's guests were to arrive was almost as warm as summer, and mindful of not casting clouts, Allegra took Susanna to sit beside her on the seat in the bowling green while she read to her.

That evening after the little girl was in bed she asked for her beloved Sarah Jane, an ancient wooden doll with faded red cheeks and one painted eye almost kissed away, and after Allegra had looked for her without success she remembered that she had left her on the seat by the tulip tree.

She refused to believe that Sarah Jane would be safe there until the morning: a big black crow might come and carry her off, and her beloved would be lost to her for ever, and as tears threatened Allegra promised to go and fetch her.

The light was going but it was still not too dark to find her way and she flung a shawl over her thin black dress and hurried down to the bowling green once more. She was returning with the doll in her hand when Oliver stopped her at the wicket gate. He did not move as she approached and with her heart sinking she hoped that he was not going to be tiresome again.

'I followed you because I can never see you alone,' he said, his easy smile sure of her forgiveness.

'That is scarcely surprising,' she said stiffly. 'I am employed here as your sister's governess, Lord Fetherstone, not as yours!'

'I wish you would not be so sharp with me. A number of my friends are coming tomorrow and an aunt and cousins to entertain them, and I shall not have a chance of speaking to you while they are here. I meant no harm the other night: it was all a piece of fun, and I thought you would take it that way, give you my word.'

'It was of no consequence.' She waited for him to move from the gate, gathering her shawl closely about her because the air was cold outside the sheltered bowling green. 'I will say good night, my lord.'

'Will you not take a stroll in the gardens with me before you go in? It is too lovely an evening to spend cooped up in a stuffy schoolroom.'

'My shoes are too thin for walking, thank you, my lord, and Miss Susanna is waiting for her doll.'

'She can wait a little while longer. Why are you so unkind? Can it be that you are afraid of me? I assure you that you have no reason to be.'

'I am not in the least afraid of you, my lord, but I

cannot allow you to jeopardize my position here as your sister's governess.'

'Now how could I do that?' There was no doubt that he could be charming when he liked, but she promised that he would not charm her. Pedestals and porcelain indeed!

'All this talk of strolls in the gardens at this time of day!' She waved her hand contemptuously towards the terraced gardens dropping down to the valley. 'Servants notice and talk and her ladyship will soon learn that her son takes strolls with her governess in the evening. I will have none of it. This is my first engagement, forced on me through circumstances, and I do not wish to leave Fetherstone, but if you will not leave me in peace that is what I shall do.'

'My mother will not believe you,' he said lightly.

'I know she will not. She will no doubt imagine that I've been encouraging you.'

'But nothing could be farther from the truth. You have encouraged me as much as a rabbit encourages a ferret.' He laughed, and then as she did not appear to share his amusement he continued half-seriously, 'I believe you are doing your best to make me fall in love with you, and you are succeeding remarkably well.' Then, as she drew away from him quickly, 'You need not fear. It is not contagious!'

'It is not indeed.' Her eyes met his with anger and contempt. 'In fact you are making me dislike you heartily. I do not indulge in idle flirtations with my employers' sons, and I will not be trifled with, my lord. Neither will I remain here for your amusement – or should I say sport? Let that be understood between us.'

There was no mistaking her air of authority and for a moment he was confounded. Then pride came to his aid. He would show this little madam that she could not dictate to him.

'We shall see about that,' he said, and before she knew what he was about he caught her round the waist and kissed her on the lips.

She twisted herself free and ran off with Susanna's doll under her shawl, and directly she had tucked it down beside her charge and kissed her good night she went to her room, locked the door and threw herself on her bed to indulge in a flood of tears.

So that was what Lady Alicia had meant when she warned her against taking such a situation in a household as large as this. If she had wanted to go out as a governess it would have been far better to endure the ill-bred manners of some rich railway baron's wife than insolence from her own kind. If Oliver Fetherstone had met her in a friend's drawing-room his behaviour would have been widely different. He was merely regarding her as a girl who would not object to a kiss or two, as a pretty housemaid would not have objected. No doubt her correct reply would have been, 'Now, my lord, none of that, if you please!' accompanied by a laugh and a glance of encouragement. She felt she had plumbed the depths of humiliation and that it was a very good thing that his friends were to arrive the following day.

She was not the only one to think so. Mrs Capper had seen his lordship following the governess to the bowling green and she had not been blind to the distress in the girl's face when she came running back to Susanna's room with the doll. She gave it as her opinion to Mrs Glynn that evening that his lordship was up to his old tricks with the new governess.

'She don't encourage him, mind,' she added. 'Nobody could say that she did. But she's a real lady, is that one, and it will be a bad thing if he don't leave her alone.'

'Calf-love, that's what it is,' said Mrs Glynn consolingly. 'Just calf-love, Mrs Capper. Think no more of it.'

.   .   .   .   .

Lady Maria Huckley, being the wife of a country squire, was accustomed to having young governesses in her household. Grand ladies like Miss Scrimger were not for her. On the morning after she arrived at Castle Fetherstone she made her way to the schoolroom and although not sufficiently interested in the governess to ask anything about her family, she saw for herself that she was a quiet, well-mannered girl, that she evidently knew her place, and that little Susanna had developed an affection for her. She supposed some might call the girl pretty, although she did not care for red hair, and the brown dress was so shabby that she wondered if she would be offended if she offered her one of Miriam's old muslins when they left. It would have to be a very old one, or Miriam's maid would be offended. She left the schoolroom quite satisfied with her sister's choice and as the days went by nothing happened to overset that opinion.

Oliver was now occupied with his friends, and the evenings were filled with dinner parties and small dances, while Lady Fetherstone's friends gathered to entertain her sister with local scandal, and their daughters flirted with young Lord Fetherstone and his friends.

The corridor outside Allegra's room became the meeting place for the ladies' maids, who broke off their gossip to stare at her as she passed and did not dream of standing aside for her on the narrow stairs. It was this behaviour that brought home to her once more the bitterness of her situation. The large rooms to which she had looked forward were not hers to enjoy. Her place was in the schoolroom behind a closed door.

After the crows had escaped with only a slight reduction in their numbers and no abatement at all in the noise of their parliaments in the elms beyond the stable block, the activities of the sportsmen became more varied, with hare-coursing, and fishing in the river below the beechwoods.

The house party gave itself up to enjoyment, and every evening Nurse Capper dressed Susanna in a party dress and Allegra was required to change into her thin black dress in order to take her charge down to the drawing-room for half an hour before the gentlemen joined the ladies. Susanna was a pretty child and a great favourite with everybody, and having seen her into the room and made her own curtsey to the ladies assembled there, Allegra withdrew to a corner with her tambour work until it was time to take the child upstairs.

She did not pay much attention to the ladies there, except to see that they were of the class on which she had turned her back, and she tried not to listen to their conversation, although once or twice she caught a glance in her direction and a whispered explanation from Lady Maria, followed by a softly spoken 'poor thing'. She was thankful when the last evening came and the next day his lordship and his guests left Fetherstone. Oliver was to travel with one of his Oxford friends to Derbyshire, where the young man owned an excellent trout river, and before she left, in writing to her sister Grizelda to tell her of her visit, Lady Maria said that with reference to a Certain Matter in her opinion there was Nothing Going On at all.

Allegra was able to settle down again with Susanna to their previous ordered existence and she was glad of it. More than once among the guests she had seen ladies who had known her mother, but they made no sign of recognition: a governess was a better disguise than she had realized.

In the meantime the closed door, from being an insult, had in some strange way become a refuge and she was thankful to find herself behind it.

9

One afternoon in late April Allegra took Susanna to tea with the children at Manning Place, as the Spenders had sold their London house and were remaining there for the summer. She could not help observing how shabby the house was and how ill-kept were the grounds, and Miss Troy confided to her that Sir Giles had spent far too much on pleasure when he was young and was paying for those pleasures dearly by a sadly diminished income.

'Lady Spender is always telling him that she needs new furnishing and more servants, and I believe Sir Giles is at his wits' end to know which way to turn.'

'Is Lady Spender extravagant?' asked Allegra.

'She has never known what it is to be otherwise,' said Miss Troy simply. 'She comes from one of the richest families in England and I have been told that after her marriage the large fortune she brought with her melted as quickly as Sir Giles's own, and that now, when it is too late, he is desperately investing in railway shares to try and recoup some of it. I am very distressed about it, Miss Lakesby. There is a gentleman in similar circumstances in my father's parish who has recently been beggared in this manner, and my father says it is because money has become the god of the nation. Every piece of paper with a railway company's heading stamped on it is considered to be worth so much gold.'

In the meantime in spite of the shabbiness of the house and the badly kept grounds Sir Giles appeared to be as free as ever in spending money. A new wagonette had recently been purchased, with a quiet pair of horses, for the use of the children and their governess, and before they parted that day it was arranged that the young Spenders should drive over on the following morning to meet Allegra and Susanna at Copley's Gate and pick primroses in the beechwoods. Easter was late that year and as it was Good Friday the children were given a holiday from lessons, while Allegra had promised Mrs Glynn to take some primroses down to the Rectory for the decoration of the church on Easter Day.

As they approached the woods in a small open carriage they saw the wagonette drawn up ahead of them in the lane, and the children were gathered inside Copley's Gate in a state of great excitement. As soon as they saw them the eldest Spender boy, Joseph, shouted to them to come quickly, and catching some of his excitement without knowing what caused it, directly their carriage stopped Allegra lifted Susanna down and ran with her to join them.

Four men at some distance from them were armed with measuring chains, and a queer-looking instrument on three legs, and from the gravity with which they were examining the land below the beechwoods it was plain that they were surveyors, making a detailed plan for the new railway. A man riding a big black horse was advising them from his superior position, while two more men, one with a cart on which were stacked short lengths of timber, and the other with a similar cart holding coils of rope, followed behind them all.

'The chains are for measuring the length of the track,' Thomas Spender said. 'And that queer-looking thing is a theo-something.'

'A theodolite,' said Joseph loftily. 'It is for measuring angles.'

'And do you know,' said their sister Anna, who was Susanna's age, her eyes round with wonder, 'the man on the horse said they were going to make a tunnel under

Bending High Street, and all the rocks and earth they dig out from it are going to be used for building a bank for the railway to run on, and that it will be higher than Bending church spire!'

The plotting of the track had progressed for some distance, and Allegra and Susanna stood with the others, watching the activities of its planners with interest. As the surveyors moved on, so every few yards a stake would be taken from the first cart and hammered into the ground, the man on horseback directing where it should go, and then a length of rope would be strung between it and the last.

The broad shoulders of the rider seemed familiar but he was too far off to be recognized, and Allegra was more interested in the railroad that was to traverse the meadowland. The eager little boys told her that it would be the width of a turnpike, or possibly even two turnpikes, set side by side.

'I expect,' said Thomas solemnly, 'there will be railways all over the world soon.'

He was told that there were railways already in many countries besides England.

'How I would like to build railways when I'm a man!' sighed Thomas.

'Master Thomas!' Miss Troy was shocked. 'Such work is very well for working men or for engineers, like that man on the horse over there, but not for you. You are the son of a gentleman.'

'And I wish,' said little Percy, the youngest of them all, 'that they would build a railway right across our park and up to our front door.'

'But your papa's beautiful park would be ruined.'

'I don't suppose he would mind,' said Percy stoutly. 'Do you know, Miss Lakesby, that horse is called Bucephalus, because the man who is riding him was the only one who could tame him – like Alexander's, you know.'

It was difficult to persuade the children to desert the fascinating study of the railway track for the purpose of picking primroses, but they were eventually induced to begin their task in the woods, still chattering about the railway however, and in consequence the basket that Allegra had brought with her was less full than she had hoped it would be when she left it at the Rectory on the way home.

About a week later she had a long letter from her Aunt Bell in which she told her that a friend of Rose's, a Miss Farrow, had been staying at Lakesby Manor for the past few weeks. She was a pretty girl, Miss Lakesby told her niece, and as she was an excellent rider and of less weight than Rose, Robert had no hesitation in letting her ride Briony.

The news upset Allegra beyond all reason: she knew she was stupid to feel angry with Miss Farrow for riding her beloved Briony and with Robert for encouraging it. There was only one person to blame, herself. She could still be at Paragay, riding Briony twice a week at least, had not that mad desire to leave the little town overcame her.

She had just put her letter away when Mrs Glynn came into the schoolroom to ask if she might speak to her.

'Why, of course, Mrs Glynn.' Allegra put a copybook in front of Susanna and told her to practise making her capital letters while she waited to hear what the housekeeper had to say.

'It's this railroad engineer,' said Mrs Glynn. 'I don't know where to put him for his luncheon today.'

'His luncheon?' Allegra could not think why the railroad engineer should be provided with luncheon.

'Mr Duffy says he is up at daybreak and he reckons

94

he doesn't touch a bite to eat till it's dark, and seeing that tomorrow they start the far side out towards Sprackley he said he'd like to offer him luncheon today at his own house, only that's four good mile on the Bending side of Fetherstone village. I don't suppose the Fetherstone Arms have given the gentleman or his young men any meal worth eating while they've been lodging there: it's a nasty dirty place, is the Arms, these days, and the beer is very bad. It seems according to Mr Duffy that the engineer gentleman is very clever and a friend of Mr Robert Stephenson, so I said, "Let him come here to Castle Fetherstone," I said, "seeing as he's working on his lordship's land. His young men can put up with the Arms for another day," I said. Our cold beef and white bread and cheese will taste better'n anything he'll get down there in the village, and our small beer is better'n the best the Arms can offer.'

Allegra agreed, wondering how she came into the discussion. But it soon appeared that Mrs Glynn was not seeking to justify her invitation to the engineering gentleman, but only requiring her advice as to where she should put him for his meal. He was undoubtedly a cut above the housekeeper's room, and equally well below the dining-room. Then where was he to go? The house steward's room? But if Mr Duffy had been anxious to offer him hospitality he could scarcely go there.

'I was thinking of the small breakfast parlour, miss,' she said at last. 'If he was to have luncheon served to him there, would you be so obliging as to have yours with him, to see as he has a good meal? Miss Susanna won't be above taking hers with Nurse Capper in the schoolroom, I know, especially if I ask the under-cook to make her one of them lemon tarts what is her favourite.'

Susanna, who had lifted her head from her third capital B to protest, was immediately reconciled by the thought of the lemon tart and Allegra said she would be pleased to join the railway engineer at his luncheon, and as Mrs Glynn left the schoolroom and she returned to Susanna's handwriting, she reflected that in the eyes of the housekeeper she and the engineer must be of a pair – a little higher than the housekeeper's room and yet lower than the dining-room.

'Come,' she thought with an inward smile, 'I am progressing! In a little while I may be permitted to have my luncheon in the small dining-room with Susanna, when the family is not in residence!'

But directly she entered the small breakfast-parlour at one o'clock that day and saw her luncheon partner with his back to her, his hands thrust deep into his pockets as he stared out over the terraced gardens and the valley to the distant hills, even before he turned at her quiet good-day, she knew why the figure on Bucephalus had seemed familiar. This was the kindly man who had accompanied her on her journey to Bending Junction and her heart lifted as he came forward to take her extended hand in a warm grasp.

'Mr Buckhurst!' she exclaimed. 'This is a pleasure indeed.'

'It is Miss Lakesby,' he said in a tone of great satisfaction. 'When I was told that a young lady would take luncheon with me I had no idea it might be you.'

'And although you told me you would be working on this new railway,' she said, 'I did not associate you with that great horse of yours when we saw you on him a week ago below Copley woods.'

'Bucephalus is my chief means of transport,' he said, smiling. 'Stoke his boilers with plenty of oats, give him a dry stable and a rub down after he's been out in the rain and he'll be better than any locomotive.' After they were seated at the table he waited until the servants had cut the beef from a joint on a side table and placed in front of them a loaf of fresh white bread, a quarter of cheese and a jug of excellent table beer before leaving the room, and then he said with a touch of concern. 'You are thinner than you were. Are they working you too hard?'

'Oh no.' She met his concern with cheerfulness. 'I am not at all over-worked. My charge is an affectionate, dear little girl and I have grown very fond of her.'

'And the rest of the family?' His blue eyes were too shrewd for her liking.

'I have not met Lady Fetherstone yet or her daughters,' she said hurriedly. 'They are to be in London until the end of June. But when Lady Maria Huckley was staying here a little while ago she never failed to visit the schoolroom once a day after breakfast. She is very charming and I am sure her sister will be the same.'

He applied himself to his beef for a few minutes and then he said, 'I believe his lordship was here for a few weeks?'

'Yes. He was here with some friends.' Her tone was cool.

'You did not meet him perhaps?'

'Oh yes, I met him.' She tried to stop herself from blushing but did not quite succeed.

'A very handsome young man,' he went on, teasing her by his persistence.

'Some might think so, I suppose.' After a moment she added, 'I was not impressed by his looks or his manners.'

'Indeed?' He saw her heightened colour and wondered in what way Lord Fetherstone's manners had offended her, but he pursued the matter no farther. The beef was good and so was the bread and cheese and the ale. He ate and drank without hurry but with appreciation, and she did not think that his table manners would have disgraced her ladyship's table.

'Mr Buckhurst,' she said, feeling as she had in the train that he was a man she could confide in, 'do you recollect that on our journey to Bending Junction you said something about hoping I would find myself on the right side of the door?'

'The door, my dear?' For a moment he was puzzled and then his brow cleared. 'Of course I remember. You allude to the door to the servants' quarters?'

'Yes. You thought, I fancy, though you were too kind to say so that I might find myself on the wrong side of it. You were correct. I *am* on the wrong side – or, at least, if I am not on the wrong side I am certainly not on the right one.'

'Neither flesh, fowl nor good red herring?' he quoted.

'That expresses it exactly.' Her face clouded. 'And I am not sure, having seen some of the family here from those quarters that I want to push the door open. I have learned a great deal about my own kind since I came to Fetherstone. The large rooms I longed for are closed to me except when I am there on sufferance as Miss Susanna's governess, and sometimes I even find myself longing for the little house that I held in such contempt in Paragay.' She tried to laugh. 'Am I not the most unreasonable of women?'

He assured her gently, trying to make a joke of it, that it was the privilege of young ladies to be unreasonable.

'Only I am no longer a young lady,' she said, her voice grating a little. He glanced at her without replying. The brown dress was certainly ugly in cut and material, but the colour suited her hair, and the lace collar and cuffs she had added to it gave charm to a very ordinary garment. She could not, whatever she wore, hide the breeding that was in her. 'Mind you,' she continued, 'some governesses are very important people. My predecessory, Miss Scrimger, was very much respected, but then she had been head-governess in a ducal household.'

'There is evidently a great future before you then,' he told her gravely. 'To be head governess to a duke's children! What more could you desire?' She saw the laughter in his eyes and she laughed with him and he was glad of it.

He stayed as long as he dared and made her laugh again with stories of the antics of her aunt's little dog Rowley, when he had met him out for a walk with his mistress one afternoon on the common behind Well Walk. It seemed that he had walked back with Miss Bell to Number 14 and had been invited in to meet Mrs Lakesby and receive her thanks for his care of her daughter during her journey. The ladies, he told her, had been very kind to him and had insisted that he stayed with them for tea.

After he had gone his cheerfulness and good sense and slow country voice remained with her, leaving with her a comfortable picture of home.

10

Whenever he could spare the time from the railroad, Mr Buckhurst found himself constantly drawn to Paragay, at first not certain that he wished to live there, and then with an increasing liking for the little town. And from the first time that he saw it as he passed it on Bucephalus, he knew that he would never find a house that would compare with the Grange.

It was exactly the house he wanted, in size, in aspect, and in setting. It was situated half a mile or so outside the town, where the road curved round towards Mayne. It was long and low and built of grey stone, with a rambling roof of grey slate, and it stood back behind a small park – a veritable miniature of a park – with a few fine trees in it. There was an old oak by the entrance gate, and there were three tall elms gossiping in one corner, while on a circle of lawn round which a gravelled drive led to the front door there stood an exceptionally fine cedar tree.

He passed the house several times during the next day or two and each time his liking for it deepened, and at last he left Bucephalus at the livery stables, changed from his riding clothes into a light coat and trousers that he felt to be more suitable for a call on a lady, and walking out to the Grange he approached the front door, set comfortably in a small porch, and pulled the bell.

A superior footman opened the door and when he told him to take his card to his mistress he looked doubtful and fetched the butler, who looked him up and down, studying his hat with distrust, and asked if Mr Cruikshank had sent him.

'Nobody has sent me,' said Mr Buckhurst, frowning.

'I happen to be looking for a house of this size in the neighbourhood and having heard the Grange may be for sale I have come to see it for myself. Kindly take my card to your mistress at once, and ask her if it is convenient that I should call on her.'

As the butler took the card from the footman the drawing-room door opened and an old lady came out into the hall. The butler put the card on a silver tray and she took it and looked from it to its owner without comment. 'Mr William Buckhurst,' she said, reading the name on the card. 'I do not think I know you, sir.'

'No, ma'am.' He stated his business once more while her shrewd old eyes studied him and did not dislike what they saw.

'The truth is, ma'am,' he ended up, 'I have fallen in love with your house. It is the sort of place I have always dreamed of possessing – a beautiful house and home.'

She smiled. 'It has been a home, and a happy one,' she said a little sadly. 'Will you come in, sir?'

He followed her into a drawing-room that did not disappoint him. It was a long and gracious room, with windows opening on to a side lawn where an ancient mulberry tree had its split sides encased in an iron corset.

'Before my housekeeper shows you the house,' she said, 'I would like to know a little more about you. I presume that Mr Cruikshank sent you?'

'If that gentleman is your lawyer then I have not met him, ma'am.' And then as she waited he plunged on, 'I am a railroad engineer, and in the course of my work I have amassed a modest fortune. I do not wish to increase that fortune by working for railways for the rest of my life. I am thirty-four and I am growing tired of the emphasis that is placed on money by those who have to do with railways these days.' He paused, looking round the room as if he were trying to see it through somebody else's eyes. 'Will you be taking all your servants with you when you leave, ma'am?'

'Not all of them. I am removing to a smaller house where I shall not need so many.'

'Then perhaps the remainder will stay on with me?'

'Are we not going too fast, sir?' His energy made her laugh. 'There is the business side to discuss first with Mr Cruikshank before anything like that can be settled.'

'I will call on him today.'

The housekeeper, a forbidding lady by the name of Mrs Potter, was summoned to show him the house and after she had taken him off Mrs Woodley sank down upon a sofa considerably shaken by her first encounter with a railway engineer, and wondering if they were all as decided as Mr Buckhurst appeared to be. She hoped she had done right to send him to Mr Cruikshank, but the lawyer was so prejudiced against railways that she feared he might dismiss their prospective buyer of her property out of hand. She would be sorry if this happened, because she had taken a liking to the big, straight-speaking man.

Mr Buckhurst returned from his tour completely satisfied: the rooms were sufficient in number and size, the kitchen quarters compact, and there was no weight and pulley attached to the door that separated them from the hall. Before the head gardener came to show him the gardens he asked Mrs Potter how many servants were needed at the Grange and she told him crisply that there were eight indoor servants, including herself and the butler, and outside there were six, the coachman, two grooms, a head gardener and two under-gardeners.

In the fruit-garden William Buckhurst was particularly interested in a hot-house built against a wall, with a fire in the wall to heat it. He gave it some minute attention and finally hazarded an opinion that it would be a simple matter to install a small boiler to heat iron pipes inside the hot-house. The head gardener told his mistress about it later, shaking his head and remarking that to his way of thinking these here railway gentlemen did not know what they were at.

Mrs Woodley pitied Mr Buckhurst as he left with the sure step of one who had seen what he wanted and intended to get it, as he still had to reckon with Mr Cruikshank. She did not know the tenacity of the engineer, however.

Having gained admittance to the lawyer's office with some difficulty, he found him to be a fussy little man, with grizzled whiskers and bushy eyebrows under a shock of grey hair, which stood on end as if he continually ran his hands through it in despair at the craft and subtlety of man. He greeted Mr Buckhurst coldly, disapproving of his hat, and when he heard that he wished to buy the Grange he asked with a superior smile if he had friends or relatives in the neighbourhood.

'I have one friend who will vouch for my honesty, if that is what is in your mind, sir,' said Mr Buckhurst stiffly. 'A Mr Jack Willoughby, whose mother resides in Well Walk.'

'Ah, the railway engineer!' Words failed to convey the contempt Mr Cruikshank felt for such people.

'You do not approve of railways, sir?'

'Approve of them?' Wrath sparkled in the lawyer's small eyes. 'Sir, they are an abomination! If I had my way every railway in this country and every man who worked on them would be sent to perdition.'

'I am sorry you feel like that, because I too am a railway engineer,' said William Buckhurst quietly. 'And I have no intention yet of going to perdition. Indeed, before such a fate should claim me I intend to purchase the Grange.'

'Ah yes, the Grange.' Mr Cruikshank eyed him malevolently. 'It has not occurred to you perhaps that it might be beyond your means? Mrs Woodley's son – Mr Quentin Woodley, the eminent Q.C. – has said that I am not to take a penny under three thousand pounds for the property.'

'There can be no difficulty about that then,' said his visitor calmly. 'As I am prepared to pay five.'

It amused him to see the astonishment in the lawyer's face. 'You mean you are offering two thousand pounds more than the price asked for it?' he stuttered.

'No price is too high if you want a thing sufficiently,' said Mr Buckhurst. 'And I happen to want the Grange.'

Mr Cruikshank tried a different approach. 'I have already had several offers for it,' he said.

'Are any of them higher than mine?'

He had to admit that they were not. 'But my dear sir,' he continued in a more conciliatory tone, 'I think you should consider the matter carefully before you proceed. You – railway people – are very anxious to become country gentlemen, and in some cases – and in some districts – this will not go down well with your neighbours. I do not mean to be offensive, pray do not misunderstand me, but there are certain standards expected of gentlemen that one like yourself might find it hard to understand.'

'I am glad you do not *mean* to be offensive,' said Mr Buckhurst, his face becoming alarmingly grim. 'You may name the price you want for the Grange and if the one I have offered is not enough I will wait until tomorrow morning for your reply. The Coach and Horses will find me until noon.' He settled the offending hat on his head with an angry bang of his fist and left, and just before noon on the following day he received a letter from Mr Cruikshank saying that he had informed

Mr Quentin Woodley of his offer and would let him know the result when he received a reply.

This was not enough for the engineer's impatient spirit. He wanted to get the thing settled and he did not trust Mr Cruikshank. His dislike of railways might be an excuse, and he could be keeping the Grange for some favoured client at the lower price. On returning to Bending Junction that day, he found several questions that had arisen over property near Sprackley to claim his attention for the next few days, but directly he had worked them out he took the next train from Bending to London and sought out Mr Woodley in his large country house in Putney, arriving late in the evening.

It so happened that he struck the gentleman in a genial mood. That day Mr Woodley had made one of the best speeches of his career in defence of an important client, and not only had it been acclaimed by all who listened to it in court, but it would no doubt be praised in most of the newspapers on the following day. He had had an excellent dinner, and some extremely good port wine to round it off, and he only kept Mr Buckhurst waiting half an hour before joining him in the library.

His visitor's quiet manner impressed him favourably, and when he was told that his call had to do with the purchase of Mrs Woodley's house in Paragay he was disposed to listen, while his puzzlement deepened.

'Ah yes,' he said. 'You must be the gentleman Mr Cruikshank mentioned in the letter I received from him this morning.'

He made a gesture inviting Mr Buckhurst to sit down and seated himself at the library table, where a small pile of papers were held together by a paperweight. He selected Mr Cruikshank's letter and read it again: the lawyer had merely mentioned that he had had an offer for the Grange from a 'railway person' but that he did not think Mr Woodley would care to consider it. He would like to recommend an offer from one of his own clients, a gentleman with friends in the neighbourhood, who had offered two thousand five hundred pounds, which he hoped Mr Woodley would consider to be a good offer.

After this second perusal he asked if Mr Buckhurst were employed in some capacity on the railways.

William Buckhurst said that he was a railway engineer and Mr Woodley considered this in silence, pressing the tips of his fingers together and examining his visitor over his spectacles as if he were about to cross question a hostile witness.

'You railway men are everywhere,' he complained. 'Can't help finding you at every step and in nearly every law-suit. Don't know why Cruikshank is so set against railways all the same. Most lawyers are waxing fat on the fortunes they are accumulating from all this litigation. But it's bad for the country of course. Carved up into iron railroads here there and everywhere, and numbers of people ruined.' His eyes rested on Mr Buckhurst broodingly. Was this, he wondered, the aristocrat of the future? This man, who had obviously come from the working classes, self-educated and now reaching up to a position beyond his comprehension? It wouldn't work, but it was no use telling him so. There was a determination in his eye and in the set of his jaw that the Q.C. had met before. He pushed the papers aside with impatience. 'Mr Cruikshank does not mention the offer you are making for the Grange. Perhaps he omitted to tell you that I am not prepared to consider any sum under three thousand pounds.'

'But he already knows that I have offered five, sir. Did he not mention that in his letter?' Mr Woodley shook his head and William Buckhurst felt his temper slipping. 'It is a pity if his dislike for railways – or possibly an interest on the behalf of a friend – has robbed Mrs Woodley of two thousand pounds.' He got to his feet and from under the brim of his hat his fierce blue eyes studied the great barrister with angry indifference. 'I want the Grange, but I will not have my business deliberately obstructed by a country lawyer. If the purchase of such a house by a person like myself is a gamble, that is my affair and mine alone. Mr Cruikshank has already accused me of wishing to be a country gentleman and that is farthest from my thoughts. I have no more wish to become such a person than I have to sit like a spider in a dusty office running up bills by delaying the completion of a client's business. I see I must look elsewhere for my house.'

Hiding his mortification as best he could, he strode to the door, not waiting for a servant to be summoned to show him out, when a word from the Q.C. stopped him.

'Not so hasty, my dear sir, if you please,' he said. 'There is some slight misunderstanding here, I think. It is unpardonable in Cruikshank not to have explained your business more fully and you may be sure I shall leave him in no doubt as to my displeasure. But if in the meantime you will let me have your offer in writing during the next few days and see that I have a draft for the money, I will be happy to settle with you for my mother's property over Cruikshank's head. He is a fool in any case, and I shall be glad when she is settled in Bath, where she may find a more sensible man to manage her affairs.' He got up and went to the bell. 'And now will you not join me in a glass of port wine before you go, to seal the bargain between us?'

It was in William Buckhurst's mind to refuse: the thought occurred to him with some bitterness that these great people were all the same. He had come across it again and again when the sale of property was being negotiated between landowners and railway companies. All offers from those they considered to be 'the lower orders' were indignantly refused until they saw that the money involved was likely to be far beyond their expectations, when they became all genial acceptance, every scruple gone down the wind. But because it was not in his nature to be ill-mannered he sat down again and accepted the offer of port wine, and drank a glass to seal the bargain, as the great man had said.

As he drove back to London in the cab that had taken him to Putney, Mr Buckhurst found that his pleasure in the purchase of the Grange had faded a little. He wondered if he had done right to buy the place, and though he knew that it was not for himself that he had bought it, he wondered if the person for whom it had been purchased would give it more than a careless glance. His victory over Mr Cruikshank was complete, but it had left a sour taste.

After he had gone Mr Woodley wrote a short and extremely sharp note to Mr Cruikshank and a longer one to his mother to say that he had accepted Mr Buckhurst's offer for the Grange. He put the letters out to be posted by one of the footmen in the morning and went back to his wife and daughters in the drawing-room, but for the rest of the evening his visitor's broad-shouldered figure and scornful blue eyes haunted him a little. He wondered what he had meant when he had called his purchase of the Grange a gamble, and he hoped that the man would be accepted by the people in Paragay, but at the back of his mind he was still very much afraid that it would not work.

.   .   .   .

Before another month had passed the news had spread round Paragay that a railway person had bought the

Grange. Mrs Woodley moved to Bath, taking with her such furniture and possessions that she could find room for in the smaller Bath house, and at the beginning of May William Buckhurst moved into the Grange, having purchased from its owner such furniture, carpets and curtains that she wished to leave behind.

He made the morning-room, which had been left fully furnished, into his sitting-room, and had his meals served in the dining-room at its large table, with an odd selection of chairs round it, and patches on the walls where family portraits and pictures had been removed.

The housekeeper, Mrs Potter, treated him with the severity she had exhibited on their first encounter, the butler showed contempt for his lack of knowledge of wines, and the new cook, engaged by the housekeeper because she was her niece, did not seem to be worth the high wages asked for her services.

In Paragay, however, when it was discovered that he was Jack Willoughby's friend, he was received with a kindness that surprised and touched him, and although many would have called upon him out of curiosity, his frequent absences from home made the chance of finding him there unlikely. And then one morning he met Bell Lakesby coming out of a draper's shop in Market Street, where she had been buying some claret-coloured purse twist for her sister-in-law.

'Dearest Laura makes such excellent purses,' she told him, her cheerfulness enfolding him in her wide smile. 'We have been so pleased that you have purchased the Grange, Mr Buckhurst. We would have liked to ask you to come in for tea with us again one day but we did not like to intrude until you are settled there.'

He asked after Allegra, saying that he had seen her once at Featherstone and had thought her rather thinner than before.

Bell hesitated. 'Her letters to her mamma and myself have been rather short of late, but then you see, in her position I do not suppose there is much to relate.' Her smile returned widely. 'But Mr Cruikshank called on us with such good news this morning that I am sure it will bring as much happiness to her as it did to us. I am going to write and tell her about it directly I have given Mrs Lakesby her twist.' She hesitated again and then went on in a sudden burst of confidence, 'As it will be all over Paragay in no time, there can be no harm in your knowing, Mr Buckhurst, as you are one of our leading residents now! Mr Barnabas Lakesby, who has always been regarded as the black sheep of my family, visited Mr Cruikshank yesterday and offered to buy Masterson's – a derelict property of my sister-in-law's – for £300! Is it not good news? Mr Cruikshank thinks it to be a very fair offer, and Mr Barnabas Lakesby would have paid over the money at once if he had not inadvertently mislaid the deeds. Mr Barnabas was extremely angry, we were told, but as dearest Laura said, it is not as if her useless land would take legs and run away. We were both most touched, though. It shows that you cannot judge people by what they may have done in the past. I think my family may have been unjust to our cousin Barnabas over the years.'

'I believe your niece told me something of this property on our way to Bending Junction,' William said thoughtfully. 'A property near Beccles, I think she said?'

'We thought it to be situated there, but we were wrong. It is in Suffolk, Mr Cruikshank says, near a place called Burston.'

'Burston.' His conversation with Jack Willoughby about a possible railway being laid in that direction flashed across Mr Buckhurst's mind. If the plan for such a railway was to go ahead then Masterson's might well be worth a great deal more than the three hundred pounds that Mr Barnabas Lakesby was so generously offering.

He parted from Miss Lakesby with his regards to her sister-in-law and to Miss Allegra when she wrote to her, and went back to the lawyer's offices in Market Square. His last encounter with Mr Cruikshank had not made him eager to see him again, but he felt bound to make sure that the black sheep of the Lakesby family did not mean to cheat Allegra's mamma.

He entered the lawyer's outer office, walking upstairs unannounced and into his private room above. Fortunately nobody was with Mr Cruikshank, but he was plainly outraged at this intrusion by the man who had already got him into serious trouble with Mr Woodley.

'Well, Mr Buckhurst?' he said, without getting up. 'I thought I had settled all the business of the Grange. I believe the deeds are now in your possession.'

'It is not the deeds of the Grange with which I am concerned this time,' said William pleasantly, taking a seat on the other side of the office table. 'I believe Mrs Henry Lakesby is one of your clients?'

'She is.' The lawyer's tone asked what affair it could be of his and William was quick to enlighten him.

'I met Miss Bell Lakesby just now in the street and she tells me that Mr Barnabas Lakesby has offered to purchase her sister-in-law's property in Suffolk – a place called Masterson's, I believe – and indeed would have purchased it outright had the deeds not been mislaid.'

Mr Cruikshank went white with anger. 'I confess they were temporarily misplaced,' he admitted. 'Entirely due to the carelessness of one of my clerks who had placed them in the wrong deed box. But they were discovered there this morning and I have written to Mr Barnabas

Lakesby to advise him that there need be no more delay.'

'Have you posted the letter?' asked William bluntly.

'No, sir, I have not.'

'Then I advise you not to post it, sir, and to mislay those deeds for at least another week while you make more enquiries about Masterson's. If it is situated near Burston it may very well be on the route of a new railway and worth a great deal more than the three hundred pounds that Mr Barnabas Lakesby is offering.'

'That is most improbable.' Mr Cruikshank dismissed the suggestion as absurd. 'Mr Barnabas Lakesby made the closest enquiries. He even travelled to Ipswich to assure himself that there could be no profit due to Mrs Lakesby from any railway in the vicinity.'

Mr Buckhurst could well believe it. 'And you have had no occasion in the past to doubt Mr Barnabas Lakesby's integrity?' he asked.

Mr Cruikshank's anger burst its bounds. 'Mr Buckhurst!' he shouted. 'What right have you to question a member of one of our oldest and most respected families? A few months' residence in Paragay gives you no cause whatever to blacken a gentleman's character.'

'I was not aware that I was blackening any gentleman's character,' said William Buckhurst patiently. 'I was only trying to protect one of your clients from being the victim of a possible fraud. Burston is situated on the route that the new line from Ipswich to Norwich is to take, but if you have had no communication from the Ipswich and Bury Railway Company about Masterson's, then no doubt Mr Barnabas Lakesby is right and it is of no value.'

He paused, watching the lawyer, who appeared to be put out by this last suggestion. In fact he was remembering certain unpleasant sentences in a letter from a well-known Q.C. as the result of his former dealings with the gentleman on the opposite side of the table, and he said hurriedly, 'I may have had a communication, but if so I have ignored it. My clerks know that any pamphlets and letters from railway companies go straight on the fire. Most of them are fraudulent and solicit investment on false promises. I do not invite my clients to ruin.'

'I can understand your dislike for railway companies as a whole,' said Mr Buckhurst smoothly, 'but if you are not prepared to take my word over this particular railway company, may I beg you to approach Mr Jack Willoughby? It was he who told me of the prospective railway between Ipswich and Norwich, and if you cannot bring yourself to mislay those deeds for a week while I make discreet enquiries that will involve nobody, I will ask him to write to you and explain the route of the railroad. You may then examine the Masterson deeds before you relinquish them to Mr Barnabas Lakesby and make up your own mind if your client will be likely to gain more from the railway than from her cousin.'

Mr Cruikshank sat silent, digesting the threat that lay behind Mr Buckhurst's suggestion. If Jack Willoughby were to be drawn into this affair and Barnabas Lakesby's offer proved to be fraudulent, it would soon be all over the town that the lawyer had made no proper enquiries about Mrs Lakesby's property, but had allowed his personal prejudice against railway companies to give the black sheep of her late husband's family the chance to rob her. He dare not risk it.

After protesting that it was a disgraceful suggestion, that he had never been asked to do such a thing before, he finally put the letter into a drawer with the deeds of Laura's property, locked it and hung the key on his watch-chain. There was no doubt, however, that he had been shaken by the interview.

'They shall remain there for a week with that letter,' he told the detested railway man in front of him. 'But only for a week, and if Mr Barnabas should enquire if the deeds have been found I shall have to tell them that they are now before me, and I shall arrange the date for the transfer of the property to him next Friday at noon. That is one week from today, and if you are not in this office before or at that time with evidence that Masterson's is worth considerably more than three hundred pounds I shall put the sale into effect without any more delay. I must guard my client's interests before anything else.' It appeared to have escaped his memory that he had not guarded Mrs Woodley's interests as well he might. 'I will give you one week to make your enquiries, Mr Buckhurst. That is the most my conscience will permit.'

'God bless you and your conscience, sir!' cried Mr Buckhurst and made his way to the railway station with all speed.

He travelled at once to see his young surveyors at Sprackley, told them that he might be away for a week, examined their plans and disposed of their queries, and set off in a post-chaise for Bending Junction. As he passed within sight of Castle Fetherstone far away on Horseshoe Hill he wondered how Allegra was faring there, and if she was finding the flesh-pots any sweeter and the dungeons less deep than when he had seen her last.

11

The railway between Colchester and Ipswich was to be opened on June 15th and from experience Mr Buckhurst knew he would not be likely to get lodgings or conveyances in Ipswich for a month beforehand. So he decided to go the other way, travelling to Brandon on the Eastern Counties Company line and then on to Norwich with the North Norfolk Company. He could make his enquiries from the Norwich end as easily as he could from Ipswich.

He arrived in Norwich late on Saturday evening, arranged for a room and a meal at the King's Head and made enquiries as to the whereabouts of the head office of the North Norfolk Railway Company. Having discovered that only clerks were there on a Sunday, he obtained the name and address of the secretary, a gentleman by the name of Moreton who had a fine house, he was told, out Wymondham way, ten miles out of the city.

He ate his dinner and went thankfully to bed and the following morning he was up early and soon after breakfast was on his way to Wymondham in a hired cab.

He arrived just as the family returned from church and on hearing his name Mr Moreton came hurrying to meet him with outstretched hand.

'Mr Buckhurst!' he cried. 'This is an unexpected pleasure. I thought you were abroad.'

'I have been home for a year or more,' William told him. 'I'd hoped you would know my name.'

'Who does not know it in the railway world?' said Mr Moreton warmly. 'You are becoming as well known at Thomas Brassey.'

'Scarcely that, sir.' William laughed. 'Brassey is one of the giants.'

He was invited to join the family at luncheon and found Mrs Moreton to be a member of an old Norfolk farming family, her father still riding to hounds. 'Though he's near eighty,' she said with a smile. 'And every time he goes out we pray that he will not be brought home on a gate. But there is no arguing with the old gentleman. He will go his own way – proper mulish.'

The family laughed and looking round at the children and the bonny wife and the pleasant master of the house at the head of the table William Buckhurst envied Mr Moreton. The butler served the table beer and the wine, while a parlourmaid handed the dishes, and poor William thought of the Grange and his menservants there and how much more pleasant was this parlourmaid than his young and clumsy footman. He thought, too, of his intimidating housekeeper, of his half-furnished rooms, and he wondered if he would ever be able to pluck up sufficient courage to tell the girl he wanted that it was all for her, that the purchase of the Grange had been a gamble for his happiness and hers.

The business he had come about waited until after the meal and then as Mr Moreton took him round his garden in the warm May sunshine William told him why he was there. The secretary's expression became more incredulous as the story unfolded and at last he exclaimed: 'You and I work for the railways, Mr Buckhurst, and we are not strangers to the greed that they inspire, but I think this is one of the worst cases of fraud I have heard. If I understand you correctly, the present owner of the Masterson property has had an offer of three hundred pounds for it from her husband's cousin, Mr Barnabas Lakesby?'

'That is correct.'

Mr Moreton was silent for a moment and then he went on: 'When the preliminary survey of the railway from Ipswich to Norwich was done we did our best to discover the owner of Masterson's but without success. We could not afford to wait indefinitely, so the plan was advertised in the local and national newspapers as usual and subscriptions came in and the shares were mostly taken up. We purposed putting the plan forward to Parliament this coming autumn, so that it might be passed in Committee in the next session. But at every turn we came upon the stumbling block of Masterson's. Nobody knew who the owner was, it had been empty for years, and though it had originally belonged to a Lady Kenworthy, she had died many years before it was let to the last tenant. Nobody knew what had become of that tenant, nor where he had gone.'

'I believe he left here without paying any rent.'

'Then that would account for him. Eventually we were told that a lawyer by the name of Cruikshank in Paragay in Buckinghamshire had the management of the estate, and we wrote repeatedly to him but had no reply.'

'I expect your letters were put on the fire. Mr Cruikshank has a fanatical hatred for railways.'

'We presumed he was dead,' said Mr Moreton, 'and then less than a month ago we had a visit from a gentleman by the name of Mr Barnabas Lakesby, who informed us that he was the owner of Masterson's and he was willing to sell – at his price – if we wished to buy it. I do not know how he knew that by this time we were so desperate to get the matter settled that we would have agreed to almost any terms, but we told him to write to the Board informing them of the lowest sum he would consider. It did not occur to us to question his right to the property.'

'And did he write to the Board?'

'We received his letter a fortnight ago. Mr Buckhurst there are forty acres at Masterson's that we must buy, and he is asking three hundred pounds an acre, as well as a further two thousand pounds for a derelict house – a mansion, as he puts it, of great antiquity. Antiquity be damned, my dear sir! The roof has fallen in and it is overrun with rats and gypsies. It is long past restoration.'

So Barnabas had asked fourteen thousand pounds for a property that he inteded to buy from his cousin's widow for three hundred. 'Have you accepted his terms?' William asked anxiously.

'We are going to accept the price for the land,' said Mr Moreton. 'But the extra two thousand for the house will come up at the Board meeting next Tuesday. Not that there is a great deal of doubt as to the outcome. We shall pay the money quickly so that our Bill can go before Parliament in time.'

They consulted about the best way of dealing with the situation, and it was arranged that William should be present at the Tuesday meeting to tell the whole story of the deception that had been practised on them to the Board. 'I wish Mr Cruikshank could be present also,' added William. 'Damned old fool – making no enquiries.'

Mr Moreton finally suggested that he should have a copy made of Barnabas Lakesby's letter making his offer to the Board on the following day. William could then take the original with him when he left on Wednesday, together with the Board's acceptance of the terms, which would be altered to an offer on those lines to the owner, Mrs Laura Lakesby – an offer of twelve thousand pounds for her land and two thousand pounds for the house.

'Oh yes,' said Mr Moreton as William looked surprised, 'when the Board realizes that the property belongs to a widowed lady in straitened circumstances they will not quibble over another two thousand. I will have Mr Barnabas Lakesby's letter and the offer from the Board ready for you to take to Mr Cruikshank's office, and while you are waiting for all this to materialize may I suggest that I send for your luggage from the King's Head and that you visit us here at Wymondham for the rest of your stay in Norfolk?'

William accepted with pleasure, and the rest of his time before Tuesday was spent in exploring the grounds and the district, in riding in the lanes and observing with interest how Mrs Moreton dealt with her housekeeping. And before he left he knew that his own house must be papered and painted and furnished too before he could ask anyone to share it with him – least of all the young lady whose image was increasingly taking possession of his mind and his heart.

He arrived back in Paragay on Thursday night with Barnabas Lakesby's letter to the railway company and their offer to Laura in his pocket, and late as it was he had no hesitation in knocking up Mr Cruikshank in his private house to show them to him.

The lawyer was in his nightshirt, the tassel on his night-cap trembling with indignation that this upstart railway person should have the temerity to get him out of bed. But when he found his spectacles and read the two precious documents the tassel shook even more with anger against Barnabas Lakesby.

'Iniquitous!' he cried. 'Iniquitous! But it is the railways that are to blame. They are the inventions of the devil, setting brother against brother, cousins against cousins. If it had not been for the existence of this North Norfolk Railway Company this would never have entered Mr Barnabas's mind.'

After another few weeks of negotiations Bell was able to write to her niece to tell her the splendid news that a railway company had bought Masterson's for fourteen thousand pounds, that the draft was already in Mr Cruikshank's hands, and her mamma wanted her to give in her notice at once to Lady Fetherstone and come home.

Allegra was delighted to hear of her mother's good fortune and would have liked to do as she said and come home without delay, but she still had not yet met Lady Fetherstone, who would not be returning to Castle Fetherstone until a fortnight before the commencement of the coming-of-age festivities, and she felt she could not consider posting her notice to her ladyship and giving her the trouble of having to look for a new governess for Susanna in the short time that remained.

So she sent her dear love to her mamma and asked her aunt to tell her that directly she met her ladyship at the end of June she would tell her that she must return to Paragay at the end of the following month. Not even to herself would she admit the delight she felt in the excuse to set herself free from Castle Fetherstone.

May had gone its way with the orchards at the house and down at the Rectory full of blossom, sheltered from freakish winds with high walls, and the hedgerows were freshly green, while in their untidy nests at the tops of the elms rooks held their noisy meetings unchecked. Mr Buckhurst's young men had been gone for some weeks now and Allegra was sorry that there was no chance of seeing the engineer on his big black horse in Fetherstone village, so that she could tell him of her mother's good news.

Gradually the Queen Anne's lace grew up round the stakes and the ropes in the meadow land where he had plotted his railway, and buttercups spread around and across it as if they would be glad to bury the project for good.

In Paragay the news of Laura's good fortune reached Eustace and he visited Mr Cruikshank to find out the truth of the garbled stories he had heard. The result of that interview was that he walked on to Number 14 Well Walk to congratulate Laura and to apologize for his brother's villainy.

'Barnabas will never be invited to my house again,' he told her. 'He intended to rob you of nearly fourteen thousand pounds.'

'But I do not think he intended it, dear,' protested Laura. 'It was most kind of him to offer me money that he could not really afford – you know how bad he is with money – and I am sure he did not realize the land was worth so much more.'

'And I am equally sure that he did,' said her husband's cousin grimly. 'You need make no excuses for him, Laura. He is a damned scoundrel, though he is my own brother, and if Buckhurst had not taken a firm line in the matter he would have been the richer by almost the whole amount that the railway company has paid for your land.'

'Mr Buckhurst?' Laura was astonished, while Bell looked up from her work with startled interest. 'I did not know that he had anything to do with it?'

'Apparently he met Bell in the street one day and in her usual way she babbled on about the money Barnabas was to pay you for Masterson's, and although I always tell you, Bell, that you talk too much, this time you talked to some purpose. Buckhurst was sharp enough to smell a rat and he went to Norwich to enquire into the whole thing, with the result that you know. It is unfortunate to have one's brother branded as a thief but that is what his enquiries proved.'

'I still feel, though, that Barnabas did not *mean* to rob me,' said Laura gently. 'He probably intended to make over any difference to me later. I am sure you are imputing to him the wrong motives, Eustace.'

'And I am sure of nothing of the sort,' said Eustace. 'But enough of Barnabas. I feel, Laura, that as a family we owe something to this man Buckhurst for his services to you. It would be a kindly gesture were you to ask him in to dinner next Saturday evening. Mary has her old Aunt Emily paying us a visit and I do not get on very well with the old lady – she cross-questions me too much. It will be a relief to leave her to be entertained by Mary and Rose that evening, while I help you to entertain Buckhurst here, thus showing him our appreciation for what he has done. One cannot reward such a man with money – I am told he is very wealthy. But I would like you to send him an invitation for Saturday if you please.'

'I will with the greatest pleasure.' Flustered and put out because she had not realized the part that Mr Buckhurst had played in the sale of her property Laura sent a note round to the Grange that evening, and the following Saturday saw her and Bell waiting anxiously in the little parlour for the gentleman to arrive. Mr Buckhurst was the first and while they waited for Eustace to join them Laura thanked him for what he had done.

'It was nothing, ma'am.' He brushed her thanks aside. 'All in the matter of business as one might say.'

'I would say rather all in the matter of friendship,' she corrected him. 'And I wish with all my heart there was some way in which I could show my thanks.'

He thought for a moment and then he said that she could help him if she would. 'The truth is, ma'am, that my house is sadly in want of wall papers and paint, besides carpets and hangings and furniture, and I do not know where to begin. If you and Miss Bell here were to be so kind as to take tea with me tomorrow afternoon I would prize the advice you could give me beyond anything.'

'But we shall be delighted, shall we not, Bell?'

'Delighted,' agreed Bell, who had been longing to see for herself if the stories she had heard about the Grange were true, and if Mr Buckhurst really lived in empty rooms with not a chair to sit on or a table to eat off.

He said he would send a carriage for them at four and then Eustace arrived and put an end to the conversation.

Eustace went home feeling that the dinner had not been wasted. The man Buckhurst had improved a great deal since the day when one of the London–Birmingham Railway Company's clerks called upon him accompanied by a young and inexperienced engineer who was at that time working under Robert Stephenson. This man, now mature and sure of himself, had a natural quietness of manner that was pleasing, and when questioned about the Grange was glad to explain his plans for the gardens and to appeal for advice.

'The head gardener has his ideas and I have mine,' he said wryly. 'And we clash.'

'I have never known a head gardener whose plans coincided with my own,' said Eustace smiling. 'And if it is peace that you want and plenty of good fruit and vegetables you will, if you are wise, not attempt to argue with him. He will see that your wife will not want for flowers either, when the time comes.' He glanced across the table at the engineer, his eyes twinkling in a way quite unusual for the serious-minded Eustace. 'One understands that is your intention in buying the Grange – to marry and settle down there?'

Mr Buckhurst flushed a dusky red but did not deny the charge, and Bell was quick to notice it and gleefully related the incident in her next letter to Allegra. Everybody, she told her, was wondering what Mr Buckhurst's bride was like, but so far no young lady accompanied by a chaperon had set foot in the place.

She then told of her visit to the Grange and how particular he had been to consult them over the decoration and furnishing of his rooms – they had been forced to take tea in a small morning-room, and had felt very sorry for the poor man. It seemed however that money was no object – although naturally they had not touched on so delicate a subject while they were there – and they had done their best to advise him that brocade was the best material for most of the walls, and for the drawing-room a Brussels carpet in moss green especially made for the room. They had explored the house with him from top to bottom, telling him where to go for his furniture and what to buy, and he had written it all down in a most business-like way. It was plain, wrote Bell, that the poor man was desperately in need of a woman to look after him. The housekeeper was like a dragon with a face that would turn the milk.

The letter had a depressing effect on Allegra. It seemed that the one man she had come to regard as a pillar, if not a rock, was to be taken from her. She remembered how kind he had been on her journey to Bending Junction, and at their luncheon together at Castle Fetherstone. She remembered too the distant sight of his figure on Bucephalus when he had been directing his surveyors in the meadows there, and now even the comfort of the chance of seeing him there had gone.

She shook off her feeling of despondency with an effort. It was her own fault that she was here at Fetherstone, cut off from everyone and from Paragay. She had chosen it, in a mad moment of revolt, and it had been a charade that had gone wrong, a masquerade that had turned sour, and it was not very comforting to consider that she had only herself to blame.

12

The Spenders had not opened their London house that year, and as a result the children were almost constantly at Fetherstone or Susanna was at Manning Place. Allegra often wondered afterwards what she would have done without Miss Troy's companionship, and from her she learned what she could have expected if she had continued in the arduous situation of a governess. She also learned what it had been like to live in the household of a poorly paid parson. Mrs Troy had died when they were all young and the eldest sister had become her father's housekeeper and companion, while looking after the upbringing of eight brothers and sisters. Miss Troy had been the second girl and from the first had been trained for a governess, her first situation being that of under-governess in a noble household.

'The post was really no more than that of a superior nursery-maid,' she said smiling. 'But I learned a great deal from the head governess and it was not long before I was able to seek a post on my own. Since then I have held such situations for the last sixteen years.'

Sixteen years of ladies' maids' corridors, of schoolroom meals, of being scolded by employers because their children were disobedient, spoilt and selfish. Allegra thought of it with horror. She learned a lesson herself, however, from Miss Troy's calm acceptance of her lot, and she determined that when she returned to Paragay she would visit the Rector's daughters more often and even help to sew their red flannel.

Now that the dividing door was open she was impatient to be through it and gone, and her solitary evenings in the schoolroom were long and lonely. But through it all she found her thoughts returning frequently to Miss Troy and how much worse her own employment at Fetherstone would have been had it been necessary for her to earn money, and not merely her own stupid pride that made it impossible for her to accept in a similar spirit the small house and the humbler friends of Paragay.

On the morning after Lady Fetherstone's return to Castle Fetherstone, Allegra was summoned to her ladyship's boudoir, where she found a little lady with dark hair under a fashionable lace cap, and a formidable air of authority. After answering her ladyship's perfunctory enquiries about Susanna's lessons and health and behaviour, she told her that she must leave at the end of July.

'You are giving in your notice?' Lady Fetherstone's black eyes looked the badly dressed girl up and down with indignation. 'Are you not satisfied here? Has Miss Susanna been naughty, or have the servants been troublesome?'

'On the contrary, Lady Fetherstone, Susanna is a darling and the servants have been extremely civil.' Allegra spoke with smiling unconcern and was about to state her reasons for wishing to leave when the door opened and Sarah followed her sister Augusta into the room.

'I beg your pardon, Mamma, we did not know you were engaged.' Augusta was about to retire again, but Sarah, after staring at Allegra for a moment, ran forward and caught her hands.

'It *is* Allegra!' she cried. 'I thought it might be when Aunt Maria told us of the colour of your hair, though she said that red hair ran in your family. But I said that none could be like yours. Allegra, my dearest Allegra, what are you doing in this – charade?'

'Allegra?' Lady Fetherstone's voice was like ice.

'Lady Alicia told me your name was Agnes, Miss Lakesby. I too feel that an explanation is due. Hold your tongue, Sarah, and let Miss Lakesby explain herself and her position in my house.'

Unwillingly Sarah dropped her friend's hands and went to stand by her mother and sister. The three of them faced her like a judge and two unwilling jurymen, with herself in the dock.

Without embarrassment she told them frankly the story of her father's death and her cousin's inheritance, of her mother's reduced circumstances that made it expedient for her to move to the small house in Paragay, and how she had longed for the large rooms and gardens that she had left at the Manor, so that she was glad to grasp at even a menial position in a big household in order to breathe again and come to terms with her new life.

'You must not blame Lady Alicia, Lady Fetherstone,' she said at the end of it. 'She refused at first to take any part in it, and my name *is* Agnes – my second name – and the only deception was that she did not tell you my history. Indeed, she offered me a home with her, but how could I accept the charity of so dear a friend? A little while ago, however, I had excellent news from Paragay: it seems that Mamma's circumstances have improved greatly, and I think that during my months here at Fetherstone I have learned to appreciate little Paragay better than I did. In any case, I intend to go home and start afresh.'

'Oh my poor Allegra!' Sarah could contain herself no longer. 'Mamma, supposing Fetherstone had been entailed when Papa died –'

'That is a nonsensical supposition, Sarah,' said her mother briskly. 'Augusta, take Sarah into my small drawing-room until I join you there. I wish to speak to Miss Lakesby alone.'

The two girls went, Sarah with one last attempt to defend Allegra that was quickly stopped by her sister. As the door closed on them, Lady Fetherstone said:

'I am sorry I did not know the truth about you. Had I done so I should probably have accepted you to teach Susanna her lessons for a time until I could find a proper governess. I conclude that if you had not had this news from your mother you would have continued to reside here under false pretences?'

Allegra admitted that this was so and her ladyship continued: 'I would be justified I think in telling you to pack and leave the house today. I do not like deception, Miss Lakesby, any more than Lady Alicia Tremayne likes it.' She paused, studying the girl thoughtfully. She was pretty, but not everyone liked that red hair and there could be no harm in yielding to Sarah and giving Allegra a few weeks' pleasure while making use of her services herself. She wrote a very pretty hand, she recollected, and she appeared to be a sensible girl, fully aware of what was due to her employer.

'I can understand that it must have been very hard for you to leave Lakesby Manor: it is a charming small country house and it is a thousand pities that it was entailed. I can comprehend, too, your feelings at the move to Paragay and the society of a small provincial town, which could not have been congenial after the society you were accustomed to at Lakesby. I shall be pleased therefore if you will stay on at Fetherstone as my guest until the end of July, when my family always moves to my father's place in Cheshire. It will please Susanna to have you here, and I am sure you have prettier dresses at home that you could have sent to you here in place of that deplorable thing you are wearing now. I will see Mrs Glynn presently and tell her to move you to a better room.'

She waited for grateful thanks and Allegra was quick

to express them, while at the same time her heart sank a little. She was to return to the right side of the door, and the ladies' maids' corridor was to know her no more. But she knew that she would rather have stayed there and continued to give Susannah her lessons in the schoolroom for the rest of the month.

She wrote to Bell, however, asking for dresses to be sent and changed from the brown dress into a grey muslin one that she had been wearing on summer evenings.

Bell was delighted to hear that her niece was to see a little social life at Castle Fetherstone before she left and she packed all her favourite gowns and slippers and lace scarves and shawls, putting in a pearl necklace and brooch that had been her father's last gift to her, and including her riding dress as her ladyship had graciously given permission for her to send for Briony.

On the first evening that she wore one of her dresses, a sea-green taffeta silk, the girls said how pretty it was and how well the colour suited her, while Lady Fetherstone studied her with a slightly startled expression. Although her hair was still neatly braided round her head the dress accentuated its rich colour, and she could see how very beautiful it was. Chestnut and gold were mingled with the red lights in it and the girl's delicate features and long dark lashes and arched eyebrows – so rare with that colouring because girls with red hair so seldom had any lashes or eyebrows at all, she could not deny that Miss Lakesby was an extremely beautiful young woman and she was glad that her susceptible son was to remain with his friends in Derbyshire until a week before the coming-of-age.

She had very little time to think of Oliver, however, in the days that followed. There were hours of consultation to be got through with Mrs Glynn about the accommodation of the fifty or more guests who were to stay at the house, the children and their nurses and governesses who might be expected, the dinners and ball-suppers that must be provided for the whole of that week, and Allegra was commanded to attend these consultations with paper and pencil ready to jot down any thoughts that might occur to her ladyship.

Mr Julian Armitage and his lordship's Oxford friends could they thought very easily be accommodated in the west wing, and to the house steward could be left the sleeping quarters for the menservants of their guests, and the agent, Mr Duffy, was holding himself responsible for the tenants' ball and their dinners eaten in tents to be erected in the park, while the village children from Fetherstone village as well as those from the estate, would have their sports in the meadows down by the river.

Each child was to have a plum bun and a glass of ale, and hundreds of pounds of beef and mutton and plum puddings and pastries had been ordered for the tenants' and farm workers' dinners.

In all these arrangements Lady Fetherstone was glad to have Allegra ready to make her endless lists and to send out invitations to those friends who were not staying in the house, and to answer enquiries that came in every day.

Her writing, she told her graciously, was much superior to that of either of her daughters, and when their schoolboy brothers arrived home for their long summer vacation it was still Allegra who was required to help her ladyship. She had a level head on her shoulders, she said, and an excellent memory.

The girls took Allegra to their hearts in their usual light-hearted fashion, and when their mamma could spare her they took her riding, which pleased her as much as it did Briony.

Susanna's capital letters were forgotten and the child

was given a holiday, old Nurse Capper doing her best to keep up with her charge's flying feet, as she followed the men who were erecting frames for the tents for the great occasion, not only in the park on the north side of the house, but on the south terraces as well for the entertainment of his lordship's relations and friends.

And among all the preparations for the great day, one morning when she was out riding with the young man's sisters she was glad to hear that Oliver did not intend to visit Fetherstone until at the most four days before his coming-of-age.

'I expect he will travel down to London first and accompany Aunt Maria and Uncle Horry and the girls,' said Sarah and she looked across Allegra at Augusta and laughed. 'Especially Miriam,' she said.

'Mamma and Aunt Maria have put their heads together,' explained Augusta, 'and they think – or at least Mamma thinks – that our cousin Miriam will make Oliver a perfect wife. In fact I have almost written her name already on the Tulip Tree.'

'The Tulip Tree?' Allegra stared and Sarah laughed. 'She does not know where it is!' she said.

'But of course I do. It is by the cottage in the old bowling green.' How could she forget that moonlit evening when a shadow had separated itself from the old tree and entered the cottage, locking the door?

'Not *that* tulip tree!' said Sarah. '*Our* Tulip Tree – the tree that Miriam drew for us when she was staying here once when we were all children. Directly we get home, Augusta, we must show it to her.'

And without waiting to change from their riding dresses when they reached the house they led her through the great state rooms, all ready for the company that was to occupy them, through the state dining-room to the great library, and from there to the red drawing-room, and the smaller green drawing-room, and through that to the small library, and then into the picture gallery, and just inside the door to the right they showed her a water colour drawing of the tulip tree. It was beautifully executed, with its white tulip-shaped blossoms all out.

'Miriam is very clever with her brush,' Augusta said. 'When Papa saw it he said it was to be our tree, and if you look into the blossoms Allegra, you will see that each blossom contains a name – our grandpapa's and grand-mamma's names at the top, while here at the bottom on the largest branches of all, there are the names of Papa's children, with Oliver's name, very large and clear, and an empty blossom next to it waiting for the name of his wife.'

'And you think it will be filled with your cousin's name?' Allegra was greatly relieved to think that his lordship's attentions would be centred on the eldest Miss Huckley during the coming festivities.

'Mamma thinks so,' said Augusta gravely but Sarah laughed.

'Do not breathe a word to anyone, Allegra,' she said, 'but we do not think that Miriam is of the same mind. You see, there is a certain captain in the Life Guards in whom she is *very* interested. He is a charming young man and very handsome.'

The sort of young man, Allegra thought wistfully, who would put a girl on a pedestal and treat her as if she were made of porcelain?

Nobody had thought to tell Oliver about Allegra's change of fortune: indeed it had not occurred to any-body that he would be interested. On finding her there-fore installed at Castle Fetherstone not as Susanna's governess but as his mamma's unofficial secretary and his sisters' friend, he did not know what to make of it.

'I thought Miss Lakesby was the governess here?' he said bluntly on the first day of his arrival.

Lady Fetherstone explained briefly about Allegra's change of fortune at home, and added that she was to return to Paragay when the coming-of-age was over. 'I confess I was vexed with her for her deception at first, but she has been most useful since I have returned home, and in fact she has been of far greater assistance to me than either of your frivolous sisters.'

Oliver found it difficult to keep his attention on Miriam during that evening: he found his eyes straying frequently to Miss Lakesby, who, after her curtsey when they were introduced, took no further notice of him.

Having discovered that the girl he had treated with such odious impertinence was indeed one of the Lakesbys of Lakesby Manor, he searched in vain that first evening for a chance to explain and to apologize, but it seemed that Miss Lakesby was as popular with his Oxford friends as were his sisters and his cousins. She was the centre of a group with Augusta and Sarah and it was obvious to his chagrined lordship that this was the society to which she was accustomed.

It was not until the following morning when he went into the small library that he found her there alone, looking for a letter from an old friend of his father's that Lady Fetherstone had sent her to find in the drawer of the table that his late lordship had frequently used for his correspondence.

Hastily he stammered out his apology. 'I cannot imagine what you must have thought of me,' he said.

'I have not thought of you at all, Lord Fetherstone,' she said cheerfully. She held out a letter to him. 'Do you think this is the one that your mamma is after? It is signed by someone who calls himself Henry and the address is correct.'

'I daresay it may be.' He took the letter and her hand. 'Allegra, tell me that you do not think too badly of me –'

She removed her hand to leaf through some more letters in the drawer. 'I think this must be the one,' she said finally.

'Are you not going to tell me that I am forgiven?' he asked.

'Oh dear, I do hope you are not going to be tiresome again!' she said with a frown. 'I assure you I was not in the least surprised or put out by your behaviour. It was only to be expected in a young man of your age and upbringing. A young governess or a housemaid, if their looks should be at all passable, are as eagerly sought as a schoolboy courses a hare.'

'But I am not a schoolboy.' He looked as sulky as one all the same.

'Are you not?' She took the letter and went to the door and there she turned to say gently, 'But I think you still have a great deal to learn.'

She was even more elusive as the day went by: her help and advice seemed to be required by everyone, last-minute notes and directions had to be written for her ladyship, embroidery patterns and novels to be discussed with the girls, sessions of listening to Euphemia's recital of her ailments and her trials with her little girls, their nurses and her servants, while Susanna was not to be neglected either. She was happy to go off, clinging to Allegra's hand, for a run in the gardens and an examination of the preparations that were now going forward in the park at full speed.

'There is to be a whole ox roasted,' she told her, open-eyed. 'And a whole sheep too!'

'Then we will pray that the weather does not change,' said Allegra smiling. It certainly seemed to be set fair but a thunder storm would not encourage the cooks who had undertaken to roast whole animals in the open.

It was during this walk with Susanna that Oliver

found her and told his sister abruptly to run on ahead as he wanted to speak to Miss Lakesby.

'What do you want to say to her?' demanded Susanna rebelliously.

'That is my business,' he said. 'Run away, Susanna, and we will catch you up in a few minutes.'

The child looked at Allegra for confirmation and she nodded. 'We will not be a moment,' she promised her. 'I am sure Lord Fetherstone has nothing very important to say.'

Susanna ran off and Oliver said quickly, 'On the contrary, I have got something important to say to you, Allegra. I can never find you by yourself for a moment and it is too bad. But you know what I said – when I was not behaving very well to you – that I thought I had fallen in love with you. Well, I am quite sure now that I am in love with you, that I am more in love than I have ever been with any girl in my life. You will not believe me, I daresay – I cannot understand it myself – but directly I saw you in that dreadful brown dress and straw bonnet I felt I'd been waiting for you all my life, that you would understand my innermost heart.'

This solemn declaration made her want to laugh, but she controlled herself firmly, wondering how many other young ladies had been told that they understood his innermost heart. 'I am sure you mean very well, Lord Fetherstone,' she said hastily, 'but you know I cannot listen to such things while I am a guest here. I believe you may be feeling some slight guilt because you treated me lightly, which, as I have told you already, was perfectly understandable, but there is no need for you to feel anything of the sort. I am enjoying my stay here in Fetherstone very much and I have forgotten all that went before, so shall we agree to say no more about it? It is as embarrassing for you to talk about it as it is for me to listen. And I can see some of Susanna's cousins bent on teasing her – I must run to her assistance.' And she left him, flying over the turf to take his sister's hand again and to lead her firmly away from some of the young tormentors who were visiting Fetherstone with their parents.

That night at dinner she found herself next to Mr Armitage, who congratulated her gravely on her mother's good fortune. 'It is good to hear of somebody who has made money out of the railways,' he said.

'But I thought, sir, that a great many people have done so?'

'There is moderation in all things,' he told her, 'and the world has gone mad. If this fellow Hudson had his way there would not be an acre left uncovered by iron rails throughout the length and breadth of England.'

'Have you met "King" Hudson, sir?'

'Only once and that was enough. He is a very vulgar fellow and I do not trust him a yard.' He smiled at her appreciatively: she was a pretty creature and an intelligent one too. 'But tell me how our railway is progressing?'

She said that the survey of the land below the beechwoods had been completed for some time, and that she had heard Mr Buckhurst and his party were now beyond Sprackley.

'Have you met Mr Buckhurst?' he asked in some surprise.

She did not mention that she had been required to lunch with the gentleman but said rather hurriedly that she and Susanna had seen him once riding his big black horse Bucephalus in the distance when he was busy with the track. 'My aunt tells me that he has bought a house near Paragay – the Grange – and that he is talking of retiring from his work on the railways,' she added.

'I daresay he has made a large enough fortune by

this time to give him independence,' agreed Mr Armitage. 'The only time I met him was in the Company's offices at Euston and he struck me then as being a capable and clever man. But these railway engineers are usually clever people. I have heard some of them give lectures at the Royal Society.'

He was then claimed by the lady on his right and Allegra was free to think what she chose.

The talk about Mr Buckhurst stayed with her, during the music that followed in the drawing-room after Susanna and her cousins had paid their half-hour visit and been fed with sweetmeats before being fetched by their nurses and governesses to bed, and when she went to bed herself in the charming little room that was far removed from the ladies' maids' corridor, she thought of what the big, gentle man had said the last time they met, his words coming back to torment her.

She was now on the right side of the door indeed, the side to which she had been accustomed all her life, but somehow now that she was back where she belonged she found herself viewing her own kind with a critical eye. Lady Fetherstone, while expressing herself as being pleased to have her as a guest, made use of her as she would not have dreamed of doing with a more exalted young lady, the girls and their cousins chattered incessantly about dress and young men, and Oliver, when he got the chance, made love to her as he would to any other pretty girl.

She looked back to herself at seventeen when her father had died. Would she not have been charmed then by the attentions paid to her by a good-looking young man like Oliver, with a title to offer her and a vast mansion like Castle Fetherstone? And would she not have chattered as thoughtlessly and as gaily as his sisters about her dresses and her conquests and the balls she had been to?

Then what could have happened to make her unkind and critical? She looked for an answer, unable to believe that her short sojourn on the wrong side of the door could have taught her such discontent, because the days when she had been a governess there already seemed to be a great way off, as if they had been passed in a foreign city.

She wished that Mr Buckhurst had been among the guests at Castle Fetherstone that night so that she could have asked his advice. She did not think that William Buckhurst was one to put women on pedestals or treat them like porcelain: he would treat them all alike and he would probably tell her not to be a goose. He believed refreshingly in speaking his mind.

13

Allegra did not find it difficult to avoid Oliver with more and more of his relations and friends arriving daily to demand his attention as their host. It is hard for a young man to make love to a girl when he is hedged around with aunts and uncles and cousins, first, second, and removed, all wishing to talk about the proposed railway and to congratulate him on his coming-of-age. Each evening there was dancing in the Great Hall for the family and their friends, an orchestra being hired from Bending Junction for the week, and Allegra did not lack for partners. Her romantic story had been made known to everyone and an endless stream of young men seemed anxious to engage her ladyship's pretty protégée while Oliver had to keep his distance, gravely doing his duty as the master of the house.

Allegra was satisfied that it should be so. It was a pleasant way to spend a summer evening, she liked dancing, and it was gratifying to wear her pretty dresses again and talk nonsense with Lord Fetherstone's Oxford friends.

The tenants' ball was to be held in the Great Hall on the night before the coming-of-age, but on the preceding night the ballroom was opened for the guests and so crowded did the room become that Allegra wondered that it could hold so many. As she turned from finishing a dance she found herself next to the hero of it all and smiled at him without thinking, and before she could turn away he asked her for the next dance.

She could not refuse, although she was dismayed to find that it was a walse, a dance that had only come into fashion two years previously with the enjoyment the young queen had found in it.

'This is a great deal more companionable,' Oliver said as he took her hand and put his other arm round her waist. 'One can talk more intimately than one can when bowing and setting to corners and taking other men's partners round the circle and so on. You are looking very beautiful tonight, Allegra. I thought I should never free myself from my plague of relations to be able to tell you so.'

She begged him not to talk so extravagantly, afraid that he would be overheard and aware that her ladyship was watching them. 'You are not very polite to your relations, Lord Fetherstone.'

'Don't do that!' he said in an anguished voice.

'Don't do what?'

'Smile at me like that. You did it just now: you will drive me demented. I adore you, Allegra.'

'If you continue in this fashion I shall be forced to ask you to take me to where your mamma is sitting. I shall tell her that walsing turns me giddy.'

'It turns me giddy to feel you so close to me.'

The expression on his face did not escape Grizelda's sharp eyes: she turned to Julian Armitage seated beside her and whispered from behind her fan that she hoped her darling Oliver was not going to fall in love again.

'Who is to be the fortunate lady this time?' His eyes followed hers to where Oliver was walsing with Allegra and he smiled.

'One could scarcely blame him, Grizel. Miss Lakesby is a very beautiful young woman.'

'I hope he will not want to marry her.'

'If he does,' said Mr Armitage consolingly, 'there is always the prospect that she will not wish to marry him.'

'What, with his position and title? A penniless girl like that? She would jump at the chance – and spoil all my plans. Maria and I have made up our minds that Oliver is to marry Miriam.'

'Have you told Miriam of this provision for her future?'

'No, of course not.' She glanced at him anxiously. 'Do you not think Miriam is fond of him?'

'Fond with a cousinly affection perhaps, but her papa tells me there are a great many young gentlemen in London even more anxious to marry her than Oliver shows himself to be, and he wishes she would select one of them so that he might expect to have his house in peace. I understand there is a young captain in the Life Guards who is a particularly frequent visitor.'

The dance finished and Lady Fetherstone beckoned to Allegra and asked her if she could find her lace scarf. 'There is a draught from the open windows,' she said.

Allegra hunted about and found it, an extremely beautiful black lace shawl, which she placed round her ladyship's shoulders, and as she did so Grizelda said that she hoped she had enjoyed her dance.

Allegra replied calmly that Lord Fetherstone danced very well and it was always a pleasure to have a good partner. 'Although,' she added, 'I am not fond of the walse. I am having the next – a cotillion – with your son Charles, and the following country dance with his brother Edward. Augusta and Sarah have been giving them lessons in dancing this past fortnight and they have improved greatly.' She moved on to find Charles and Julian told her ladyship that he did not think Oliver was in any danger from Miss Lakesby.

'I daresay she finds him too young for her,' he added.

'Too young?' Grizelda was indignant. 'She is only nineteen and he is twenty-one the day after tomorrow.'

'Possibly her family misfortunes have given her a

gravity unusual in a girl of her age. She seems older –
and wiser – than Oliver.'

'Of course,' said his companion suddenly, taken with
the truth of this remark, 'if Oliver should marry a nice
sensible young woman – with such striking looks too –
it might cure him of the habit of falling in love with
every girl he meets. It is time he grew out of it, and
I hope I shall find time to speak to him seriously tomorrow. He will have to realize the full responsibilities
of his position'.

Julian suddenly became grave. 'I've told you before
to beware of what you are about with Oliver,' he said
in a low voice. 'He will not stand much more inter-
ference, Grizel. Let him manage his affairs of the heart
in his own way.'

'Thank you Julian, but I know my own son,' said
Lady Fetherstone and Mr Armitage said that if she
would excuse him he thought he would go to the card-
room.

His walse with Allegra had inspired Oliver to disregard his relatives' gossip and raised eyebrows, and he
singled her out for the rest of the night much to her
dismay. He was forced to give the supper dance to his
cousin Ruth, the eldest daughter of Viscount Melton,
old Lord Webberley's heir, but he did not give up easily.
The night was warm and in the small hours of the morning the long windows of the crowded ballroom were
flung wide, and Allegra, who had been engaged in a
particularly boisterous country dance with young
Charles, stepped out on to the terrace to cool down. She
did not realize that Charles was no longer with her until
she turned to speak to him and found Oliver beside her
instead.

Before she knew what he was about he had taken her
hand and led her to a more secluded spot where he
asked her to marry him.

'I want our engagement to be announced tomorrow, at the tenants' ball,' he told her. 'It is no good avoiding me, Allegra. It has got to be said. I love you and I want you for my wife. You cannot refuse me.'

'You have had too much wine,' she said in the tolerant tone she would have used to young Charles. 'You will feel calmer in the morning.'

'The morning is already here,' he said. 'Can you not see the dawn breaking over the Copley hills?'

She would have dearly liked to have something in her hand to break over his head, but instead she said coolly, 'I am very honoured by your proposal but it is quite impossible. When I leave Fetherstone next week I shall return home to Paragay, and I do not intend to marry anybody just yet.'

'But do you not care for me at all?' he asked.

'Of course I care for you, as I care for your mamma and your brothers and little Susanna and Augusta and Sarah. I care for the whole lot of your nice – Tulip Tree!' She laughed and released her hand. 'But I do not wish to marry you and so I must refuse your proposal. For one thing you are too young for me. No, do not look so cross. You remember telling me once that I was too young to be a governess, and I said it was a fault I would grow out of, and now I promise you that you will grow out of yours. It may take quite a long time – five years or more – before it happens, but you will thank me for refusing you then.' And she escaped him and returned to the ballroom.

The next morning Oliver appeared in his mother's room while she was having her breakfast and drank a glass of champagne with her, while accepting the miniature of herself set in diamonds that she had made for him. 'There will not be time to give it to you tomorrow,' she told him. 'And tonight there is the tenants' ball and everyone will be giving you presents.'

'The artist has made you look very determined.' He studied the face in the miniature with care. 'But you *are* very determined, are you not, Mamma?'

'I usually get my own way,' she admitted with smiling complacency. He glanced from the pictured face to the original in silence, thinking that she had certainly had her own way with Julia, and although he was glad of it now he had been far from glad at the time.

'Allegra will make a list of your presents after to-morrow,' she went on. 'The silver tea service that your tenants are giving you is beautiful, and there is the china service from your aunts and uncles on my side of the family – one hundred and eight pieces in Sèvres china – a very handsome gift. And the diamond ring from your grandpapa –'

'You might think I was getting married instead of coming of age,' he said despondently. 'You may as well know, Mamma, that last night I asked Allegra to marry me, hoping to be able to announce our engagement at the ball tonight, but she refused me.'

'Refused you? Impossible!'

'It was my fault. I rushed my fences, and I did not behave very well when I thought she was Susanna's governess. She has not forgiven me for making free with her then.'

'But if Allegra Lakesby indulged in such an escapade she has only herself to blame.' The objections that he had foreseen were not forthcoming, however, which surprised him. The fact was that since she had discussed Oliver's admiration of Allegra with Mr Armitage the night before Lady Fetherstone had come to the astonishing conclusion that the girl might be exactly the kind of wife she required for her son. She had no money, but she came of a good family, and she was a clever girl, not feather-brained like little Miriam. Her behaviour during the last month at Castle Fetherstone had been a model of decorum, and she could see her as a daughter-in-law who would be an acquiescent companion to herself, and an unofficial secretary, answering all those tiresome letters that she did not like answering herself, and who would not dare to question her continued authority in the household. Her mamma, Mrs Henry Lakesby, could be expected to be filled with gratitude and delight to have her daughter raised to the position of Lady Fetherstone, where another more important mamma might wish to see her daughter with the full authority of Lord Fethertone's wife. On the whole it was decidedly a match to be encouraged.

'I daresay you took her by surprise,' she told him consolingly. 'When she has had time to think it over I am sure she will change her mind. I will take her to Webberley with us when we go next week. She can take her little mare Briony, or whatever the thing's name is, and you can join us after we arrive. She will have settled down by then and Webberley is so vast that when you go riding you will very easily be able to separate from the rest of the party and be on your own. You will return to Fetherstone with Allegra engaged to you, my dear: have no fear of that.'

'There are times, Mamma, when I do not know what I should do without you,' said her son, greatly encouraged. It was the last time he was to say such a thing to his mother.

The tenants' ball went on into the small hours and Allegra found that she could escape early without attracting much notice, and it was as well that she indulged in an early night because on the following morning everyone was astir at an early hour and further sleep was not encouraged by the Bending Town Band, which started up outside the north front at seven o'clock and kept it up throughout the morning, until some of the carriage horses arriving with guests were so astonished by the noise going on in the carriage sweep that they showed a tendency to bolt.

Allegra was down early to breakfast that day and there was a letter in the postbag from her aunt. Having fetched her hat, she found a secluded seat in one of the small temples that were scattered about the grounds and started to assimilate its contents in peace.

It was written in her aunt's usual cheerful style, relating the small happenings of the uneventful little town of Paragay. It also told her of Mr Buckhurst's new house, and the workmen who had been there, and the furnishers who had been moving in furniture and carpets and hanging curtains at the windows, and how some of the neighbouring gentlemen who had called on him there had been agreeably surprised with the way the house was appointed. *Although,* continued Bell, *your dear Mamma and I were not so surprised, as he had asked our advice when he first bought the house, and he seemed to understand at once when we said it should be furnished with quiet good taste. He sent a message to you, by the way. He said I was to ask if the fleshpots were sweeter and the dungeons less deep. I cannot comprehend in the least what he meant.*

Allegra sat silent with the letter in her lap: she could hear his voice saying the words, she could see the twinkle in his blue eyes. The brass band could not be heard so plainly here, but the volume of voices above and below the little stone refuge were increasing every moment. Light voices, laughing voices, lowered voices talking scandal, teasing, quizzing voices, flirtatious voices – she suddenly wished that she could run away from them all and go home and ride her beloved Briony over the familiar lanes round little Paragay.

And then her solitude was invaded: somebody entered the temple and said good morning, and she looked up quickly to see old Lord Webberley there, leaning rather heavily on a stout malacca cane, with an even stouter ivory handle to it, and studying her intently. His face was hawk-like, his figure bent, but his eyes were uncomfortably perceptive. 'You,' he said, as she put the letter away in her pocket, 'are the Lakesby girl.'

'I beg your pardon, sir?' She got up quickly, flushing, and he waved to her to sit down again.

'Old people,' he told her, 'have a licence to say what they like and to whom they like. Knew you by your hair. Lot of Lakesbys have that coloured hair. Knew one of them – Henry Lakesby. Was he your father?'

'Yes sir.' She sat down again and he sat down beside her.

'Good fellow, Henry,' he said. 'Friend of my son, Melton. Came to Webberley in the autumn sometimes. Fine shot.' He looked at her sharply. 'Going to marry Oliver?' he asked.

'No, Lord Webberley, I am not.' She wanted to ask what business it was of his, but she concluded wryly that such an impertinent question was also perhaps one of the privileges of old age.

'Has he asked you?'

'He asked me the night before last and I refused him,' she said, daring him to think what he liked and he chuckled.

'Glad to hear it. He's a spoilt pup. Not grown up yet.' He sat frowning for a moment and then he asked, 'In love with him?'

'Not a bit.' Her reply was as abrupt as his question and eyes gleamed approval.

'You'll marry him all the same if you don't look sharp. He spent some time yesterday with his mamma and I understand that she approves of his choice.'

'But I thought Lady Fetherstone wanted him to marry Miriam?'

'That wishy-washy child? No, Oliver will never marry Miriam. Needs somebody with more spirit — somebody to keep him in order.'

'Like a governess?' she suggested demurely and he laughed.

'Exactly.'

'But I do not see how I can be persuaded to marry Oliver if I do not wish to.'

'You don't know my daughter Grizel. Once she has set her mind to a thing she does not give up. Did you know that you are to come to Webberley with them all next week?'

'I think you must be misinformed, sir. I am going home to Paragay.'

'I see you do not yet know my daughter. Underneath that charmin' way of hers there is a will of iron. If she sets her mind to a thing nothing will shift her. Take this railway for example. Do you know why she has given way so gracefully to Oliver lately, agreeing that it will not be at all unsightly or spoil the view across the valley? It is because she has been enlisting the help of certain members of Parliament in London to see that the Bill for the railway is thrown out in Committee. The most influential of them, Sir Gilbert Buttrell, is to be here today, and he has given his word that it will be done.'

'But people will have invested in the railway by this time, surely?' Allegra felt suddenly afraid. 'Will not the shareholders lose their money?'

'I daresay they will.'

'But that would be monstrous. Can nothing be done? Can your lordship not persuade Lady Fetherstone that it will mean ruin to many people if the railway should be abandoned at this late hour?'

'My dear, nothing will persuade Grizel to do something she does not wish to do. She does not want the railway, therefore she will not have the railway.'

'She will not care if people are ruined?'

'Not a whit.'

Allegra set her chin. 'She will not make me marry Oliver.'

'She will unless you make a fight for it. My dear young lady, if you don't look sharp your name will be on that ridiculous Tulip Tree of theirs before you can say knife.' He saw the doubt on her face and put his dry old hand on hers. 'Very persuasive is my daughter Grizel – very full of charm. "Now, Allegra," she will say, "you know you are in love with my darling Oliver, and think how pleased your dear mamma will be –" She will bring out all her guns and after a month of such bombardment at Webberley you will be helpless. Unless you escape first.'

'Escape?' Her dark eyes met his questioningly.

'Yes. You will have to make a bolt for it.' He chuckled as voices were heard, coming in search of him, and he got up and offered her his arm, and she took it with a word of thanks. 'Don't forget,' he murmured just before his daughter joined them to scold him for running away and to tell Allegra that a number of people wished to meet her. The Tulip Tree was already claiming her as its own, and as Lady Fetherstone led him away the old gentleman turned to wink at the girl as if he read her thoughts.

. . . . . .

Mr Buckhurst was passing through Fetherstone village from Sprackley that morning on his way to Bending Junction where he hoped to catch a train to London, and Bucephalus being as astonished as the carriage horses at the noise of the bands that were now playing in the park, his owner asked the landlord of the Fetherstone Arms what was going forward. He was told that it was the much anticipated coming-of-age of the owner of Castle Fetherstone, and as the whole village was closed and shuttered and there was little prospect of getting anything to eat or drink that forenoon, he left Bucephalus to be baited and rested and made his way on foot towards the great mansion on Horseshoe Hill.

Having reached an advantageous position below the lodge gates he leaned his arms on the top bar of the park fence and studied the scene with amusement and interest. Above him, as far as the entrance to the north front, marquees and tents had been set up as if for a fairground. Crowds of children and villagers, besides tenants and their families from the estate, were clambering down from wagons and carts and gathering in greater numbers every minute, converging on the spot where an ox and a sheep were being roasted for their dinners in the larger of the tents. He had no doubt that on the south terrace grander tents waited for the entertainment of the friends and relatives of his lordship, gathered there to congratulate him on having attained his majority and independence that day.

Buckhurst's thoughts went to Allegra, wondering if she was among the smartly dressed crowd who would be thronging the south terraces and he wished he had the courage to go and find her, but for the fact that he might pose some major-domo with the problem of what to do with him. Should he be requested, as a railway person, to return and join the tenants in their roast beef and beer, or should he be invited to mingle with the guests and eat strawberries and cream and drink his lordship's health in champagne?

He had got thus far in his fancies when a voice suddenly hailed him. 'Hey!' it said. 'You there, Buckhurst, or whatever your name is. Come here – I wish to speak to you.'

He turned and saw the choleric countenance of Sir Giles Spender whose carriage, along with a few other late comers, was climbing the road to the house.

'Sir?' William Buckhurst was not best pleased at being treated with such lack of courtesy and showed it.

'Well, get in, man,' said the baronet testily. 'Don't stand there gaping. My carriage is blocking the way.'

As the groom did not descend to open the door for him Mr Buckhurst had to open it for himself and got in, seating himself opposite Sir Giles and his lady. The latter, who was not introduced, stared at him from under her parasol for a moment and then looked away as if he were not there.

'You are the engineer on the Bending Junction–Worcester Railway,' said Sir Giles. 'Give you some advice. That railway will never go through the Fetherstone land: her ladyship will not allow it. I hear she has got Sir Gilbert Buttrell here today, and she will get a promise from him that he will see that Bill thrown out in Committee. Charmin' woman, but devious. Damned devious. Know her well. There is no chance of taking your railroad through the Fetherstone property'.

'I beg your pardon. I thought the land belonged to Lord Fetherstone?'

'And he will do exactly as his mamma tells him. No, that Bill will be thrown out if it takes that route.'

'But if it were to go through the Spender property will it still be thrown out?'

'That would be a different matter, but the price of my acres is increasing every day that you delay, and I would advise you to tell your people to hurry.'

William said he would be seeing the Chairman of the Board for the Bending Junction–Worcester Railway Company that week and he would put it before him.

'If he fights shy of it,' said Sir Giles, 'tell him that

not even Hudson would defeat Lady Fetherstone. She will not let it go through.'

'You think so, sir?'

'I know it.' The carriage had reached the lodge gates and Sir Giles told his coachman to stop. 'They'll be waiting for you up there,' he told Mr Buckhurst with a nod at the crowded park.

Mr Buckhurst doubted it, but he jumped down from the carriage, took off his hat to Sir Giles and his lady, shut the carriage door and watched them drive on.

What did that self-important gentleman know of Hudson? he wondered. A sparring match between Lady Fetherstone and 'King' Hudson might have its amusing side, but in the meantime it would delay the building of the railroad by at least a year, and the interests of the shareholders came first. The Spender land was the alternative, and it seemed that the Spender land it must be.

14

William Buckhurst followed the carriage through the gates between the lodges, and as there was nobody about to challenge him, he walked on up the road until he had left the stable block on the left.

Here the carriage way swept round past the east wing to the north front, but he had no wish to continue in that direction. He discovered a small path leading down through a shrubbery to the left, and as this appeared to be in the opposite direction from the park where the bands were playing loudest and it was cool and shady, he took it, and followed it to a door set in a high brick wall. Beyond the wall there were children's voices, and connecting such sounds with Allegra he tried the door, found it unbolted and pushed it open, and found himself in a garden, enclosed by the same brick wall. In one corner there was a cottage in the shade of an old tulip tree, and on the lawn in front of the cottage half a dozen small boys were playing cricket. A lot of little girls were racing about getting hot and excited while the Spenders' governess and several nurses did their best to quieten them.

Through an iron gate in the middle of the wall to the west of the garden he caught glimpses of gaily dressed people, and he could hear another band playing in the distance, and as he stood there, ready to beat a retreat, the iron gate was opened and a girl came down into the garden to greet Miss Troy.

It took William a minute or two to recognize her in her dress of embroidered muslin and her white silk bonnet trimmed with cornflowers and ears of corn.

Then little Percy Spender saw him standing there and came running to ask him if he had come to start making the railway. He told him it would be a long time before that happened, but he threw his hat down and caught the little boy up and perched him on his shoulders, and thus holding him lightly by his legs he took him back to his governess. As he lowered him carefully to the grass and straightened his back he found himself looking into Allegra's smiling eyes.

'Mr Buckhurst!' She was glad to see him. 'I did not expect you to be here today.'

He said something about wanting to see his lordship about a small matter, having forgotten the importance of the day. 'But my business will wait,' he added, 'I am sure he will not wish to discuss railway plans today.' He turned back to fetch his hat from where he had left it and she walked with him. 'I hear from your aunt that you have been invited to stay on here as her ladyship's guest,' he said gravely, adding with a slight smile, 'on the right side of the door.'

'Very much on the right side,' she said wryly. 'I think my stay on the wrong side for the last few months has made me too critical of my own kind, Mr Buckhurst.'

'Yet you are looking very happy – much happier than when I saw you last,' he told her. She was also looking extremely pretty, and he regretted the plain brown dress. In her muslins and silk bonnet she had taken herself back to where she belonged: the little governess had perhaps been within his reach, but this smart young lady put a doubt into his heart. It seemed she might be far beyond it, and he had lost his gamble before half the dice were thrown.

While he remained silent she said in a low voice:

'Mr Buckhurst, I need your advice.' There was no time to be reticent, the thing had to be told. She went on, the words coming with a rush, 'Lord Fetherstone has asked me to marry him, and his mamma thinks, oddly enough, that I would make an excellent wife for her eldest son.'

He could see nothing odd about that, but all he said was, 'And do you agree with her?' Waiting for the answer that was to shatter his hopes finally.

'No, I do not.' Her emphatic tone gave him encouragement. 'I have already refused him. But she has made up her mind that I am to go with them to Webberley next Thursday and I am afraid that when I am there I shall be at her mercy. You know the old story of drops of water wearing away a stone? That is what is will be like with me. Her father, the old earl, warned me of it this morning and I believe him. In the short time I have known her I have learned that her will can be like granite.'

This was an echo of what Sir Giles had just said about her ladyship but the girl beside him had shown spirit enough in the past and he frowned as he asked her if she could not tell Lady Fetherstone that she must return to her mamma.

'It would be no good. You do not know her. She would simply brush it aside and say that she could well spare me for another few weeks.'

They came to where he had left his hat and he picked it up and turned it about in his hands for a few minutes, before he said, 'You will be packed and ready for the journey by Wednesday I take it?'

'Oh yes.'

'Then all you have to do is to write to Mrs Lakesby tomorrow telling her that you are travelling home on Wednesday morning, and on that same morning inform her ladyship that you are expected home that day, and request a carriage to take you and your luggage to Bending Junction to catch the next train to Paragay. Her ladyship may be a determined lady, but if my memory serves me right, Miss Lakesby too can be very determined when she likes to be.'

'It sounds very simple when you put it like that.' For a moment her face brightened, and then she remembered her little mare. 'But Briony? She is here with me. What shall I do with her?'

'Ask one of the grooms to take her to Bending Junction at the same time. There must be plenty of grooms in those great stables that I passed just now.' His eyes rested on her thoughtfully. If these great folk were determined to have her in their family, who was he – a mere railway engineer – to say that they were wrong? He thought of the Grange and its contents, purchased with only one thought in his mind, and it was small and insignificant beside the great mansion of which she would be the mistress if she married young Lord Fetherstone. 'Do nothing in a hurry,' he said gravely. 'You may change your mind long before Wednesday comes.'

'I shall not change my mind,' she said, and then voices calling her made her turn her head, and she saw Sarah push open the iron gate and come into the garden, and beyond her the cottage and the hateful tulip tree. That dreadful tree of whose blossoms she was destined to make one.

She said a quiet goodbye and went to meet Sarah while he crammed his hat on his head and returned by the way he had come.

'Mamma sent me to find you,' Sarah said breathlessly. 'Who was that man?'

'Mr Buckhurst.'

'Oh, the railway person. I suppose he came the wrong way and wanted to be directed to the park? If he has come for Oliver's signature to his stupid railway plans he won't find him ready to do anything of that sort today.' She took Allegra's arm and bore her away, back to the throng of guests on the terraces below the south front, and as they went her captive felt that the tulip tree was reaching out its very branches to claim her.

She had hoped that Mr Buckhurst might come to her help and be ready with advice, but instead he had stood aside and left her to fight her battle alone.

.   .   .   .   .

As he reached the lodge gates again on his way back to the Fetherstone Arms William Buckhurst met another carriage with an important-looking gentleman in it. He thought he recognized him as Sprackley's Member of Parliament, and he remembered Sir Giles's warning once more. He stood back to let the carriage pass and the gentleman leaned from the carriage and said 'Thank 'ee, my man,' and gave him half a crown.

William tossed it, bit it, and put it in his waistcoat pocket for luck before going on down the hill to fetch Bucephalus and continue on his journey to Bending Junction.

If he meant to save the railway, he thought, he might have to work fast. His young surveyors were already heading across country towards Evesham and Worcester beyond: he must leave for London immediately and put the final plans, re-routed through the Spender land, before the Board.

He left Bucephalus in his usual quarters in Bending and in the days that followed while his thoughts were entirely occupied with the railway, at Fetherstone Allegra found herself treated with as much deference as if she were already engaged to Oliver. On Sunday morning, when she accompanied the family to church, she had been required to sit beside him in the square family pew, and to share his prayer-book, while the villagers craned their necks to see the romantic young lady who had been a governess up at the house and was now going to marry his lordship.

It was an un-nerving experience, and Allegra was thankful that his lordship was to leave for Scotland the following morning, and only held her hand a moment longer than was necessary in parting as he promised her that they would meet again at Webberley.

By Tuesday she had heard so much about the excellence of Oliver from his mamma, and the exalted history of his family from the girls as they conducted her round the house and returned to the picture gallery, giving arch glances at the wretched painting of the tulip tree as they passed, that she knew she could bear it no longer.

She made the excuse of a headache that night and went to her room early so that she could plan what to do. She knew she would be no match for Lady Fetherstone in spite of what Mr Buckhurst had said, and as she sat staring at the empty trunks, ready for the maid to pack in the morning, ideas began to formulate in her mind. Her name had been freshly painted on the lids in large white letters, and beneath them were the labels written in Aunt Bell's sloping hand: *To be Left at the Parcels Office at Bending Junction until called for.* She had only to alter Bending Junction to Paragay and they would be ready for the railway.

Supposing she packed the trunks now, this very night, leaving them to be despatched later on? She could slip down early in her riding dress and her hat with the veil and her riding gloves, and ask one of the grooms to saddle Briony for her as she fancied a morning ride before breakfast. Then she would ride her to Bending Junction and find in the town some groom from a livery stables who would be willing to accompany her mare in a horse truck on the railway to Paragay, while she travelled in the same train in a carriage in front.

The more her agile mind considered the prospect the more attractive it became. She would leave a letter for Lady Fetherstone, thanking her for her hospitality and asking for her luggage to be sent on to her, and by the time her ladyship received it she would be on the train travelling with Briony to Paragay.

Hastily she set to work on the trunks, throwing her clothes in at speed, emptying the cupboards and the drawers and shelves in her room and moving as quietly as she could. She was sorry not to be able to say good-bye to Susanna and Mrs Capper but she dare not risk her intended flight being discovered.

It was not long before the trunks were full, the lids closed and strapped lightly, and then before her candle burned itself out she wrote her letter to Lady Fetherstone, thanking her, sending her love to Susanna, her regards to the rest of the family not forgetting Lord and Lady Webberley, and signing herself, *Affectionately, Allegra Lakesby*.

Her preparations complete she slept but fitfully, afraid of over-sleeping, and woke at daybreak and got up and washed and dressed. Once in her riding-habit she felt safer: anyone seeing her would think nothing of a morning ride. She waited until she heard the servants moving about the house and then she made her way to the east wing and the stairs leading down to the side entrance. From there she walked quickly to the stable block and told a groom to saddle Briony, but when the man came back with the little mare he was at first unable to believe that she intended to go riding alone.

'Her ladyship would wish you to have a groom with you, Miss,' he told her.

'I shall not be going far,' she replied smiling. 'Just up over the hill and back, and Briony is surefooted. I do not wish to have any groom with me, thank you.'

He watched her go with misgiving, in spite of the

half-sovereign she gave him for his care of Briony, and she rode down the road to the lodge gates for what she hoped was the last time. As she glanced back at the great house she could see that the shutters of some of the apartments were open, but those where the family slept were all fast shut.

Once past the lodges she put Briony at a canter down the road, skirting the village when she came in sight of it by a stretch of common land and joining the Bending road when she could be sure of the shelter of the beech avenue.

Briony went happily, as if she knew she was going home.

.   .   .   .   .

Having said what he had to say to the Chairman of the Bending Junction–Worcester Railway Company and obtained the Board's agreement that the Spender land would be a safer investment than that of Fetherstone, Mr Buckhurst took an early train from London that Wednesday on his way to Birmingham, intending to travel from there to Worcester, and having reached the Junction he happened to glance out of the carriage window and saw a young lady in a riding dress, with Briony's bridle over her arm and Briony herself standing patiently beside her, while she argued with a porter, her veil flung back and her flushed face and sparkling eyes showing a vast amount of temper.

Mr Buckhurst seized his valise and jumped down from his carriage to join her. 'Good morning, Miss Lakesby,' he said pleasantly. 'May I be of assistance?'

She turned to him with relief. 'It is this stupid porter,' she said indignantly. 'He tells me that he cannot put Briony on this train.'

'As it has only passenger carriages I do not see how

he can,' agreed William Buckhurst. 'I am afraid Briony will not be able to travel on it, even in an open third-class.' He looked about him. 'Where is your groom?'

'I have no groom,' she said crossly. 'I intend to travel with Briony in the horse truck or whatever it may be called.'

'That is quite impossible.' He dismissed the suggestion as absurd. 'It needs an experienced groom to travel with a horse, my dear young lady. A sudden jolt might throw your mare, and if you were unprepared for it she might fall and break a leg. You do not wish to risk Briony's life, I suppose, even if your own is of no consequence to you?'

'I asked for a groom to accompany me at the livery stables here,' said Allegra unhappily. 'But they had not one to spare and they were very uncivil about it. They said that as the railways had taken most of their trade they were not going to help me to rob them of what was left.'

'I am not surprised. Livery stable owners are not very helpful to railway travellers. I suppose Lady Fetherstone refused to send a groom with your mare?'

'I did not ask her,' said Allegra looking rather ashamed.

'But – where is your luggage?'

'Still at Castle Fetherstone I am afraid – I just ran away.' Her eyes were lifted to his beseechingly. 'Don't think too badly of me, Mr Buckhurst. I had not the courage to face Lady Fetherstone as you suggested. I knew she would defeat me. So I packed my trunks last night and early this morning I had Briony saddled and rode to Bending. But I thought all railway trains had horse trucks?'

'Not all of them. But we will allow this train to go, shall we, while I see what I can do. Have you breakfasted?'

'Oh no.'

'Then I will have a word with my friend Berry, the stationmaster. I used to lodge with him in his house here at one time and his wife is an excellent cook. I will see if she cannot provide you with breakfast while I find a groom for that mare of yours.'

He told the porter to make Briony fast in the parcels yard and he took Allegra across to the stationmaster's house, a charming little house with a neat garden, and here she was presented to Mrs Berry, a rosy-cheeked country woman, who said that of course she could give the young lady breakfast. 'And you too, Mr Buckhurst, if so be as you want it,' she added.

He said he might join the young lady later for some coffee and he left Allegra to be conducted to a small parlour, with a print of the young Queen in her coronation robes, with the rose of England at her feet, over the fireplace. Under her serene gaze Allegra removed her hat and veil and did full justice to the cold ham and fresh eggs and steaming coffee and bread and butter. She was just finishing as Mr Buckhurst came back and for a moment his eye was caught by the morning sunshine that was pouring through the window of the little room and turning her hair to red gold.

'Is his lordship still at Fetherstone?' he asked as he sat down at the table opposite her and accepted a cup of coffee.

'No. He left on Monday.'

'So that he is not likely to be out in hot pursuit after you. I presume you did not tell her ladyship that you were departing before you left?'

'No, I wrote a letter to her.'

'Pinned to your pincushion? I am told that is the way heroines of most novels behave.'

She flushed angrily under his amused eyes. 'I wish you would not treat it so lightly,' she said.

'I beg your pardon.' But his lips looked as if laughter was still not far from them. 'I have found a groom for Briony. He is a man who has often accompanied Bucephalus for me and he can be depended on. The stationmaster will see that there is a horse truck attached to the next train.'

'Thank you.' Her dark eyes met his with the anger suddenly quenched. 'I know you must think me silly to behave like this, and it was not an easy decision to make. I daresay I shall be laughed at in Paragay, regarded as the prodigal daughter coming home, much chastened by her experiences.'

'You will never be chastened by anything,' he told her smiling. 'I'll warrant you were a rebel from the day of your birth.'

'I was not a rebel until we left Lakesby – although I do recollect a birch rod that hung over the fireplace of my nursery and that it was not spared if I misbehaved.' She laughed suddenly which seemed as if her conscience, awakened by her ingratitude to Lady Fetherstone, was now back to its natural state. 'But when we first moved to Paragay I could not endure it,' she added.

'Now I wonder why?' He became thoughtful. 'To me it is a very charming little town, filled with kind and gentle people. I have known Mrs Willoughby for many years – her son Jack is one of my best friends – but I did not expect the welcome I have had from others there. There is an old Major in Well Walk for instance: he has frequently had me to his house for games of backgammon, and he has told me of the best winemerchants in the town. Then there is your cousin, Mr Eustace Lakesby – he has not hesitated to advise me on the volumes I should purchase to fill my library shelves. The only books I possessed were a few classics left me by an old friend, the parson of the village where my father was the wheelwright, and some scientific works of interest only to myself. But your cousin has done more than that: he has taken me as his guest to several lectures on scientific matters in the town, some extremely interesting. And then of course there is your mamma, and there is your aunt: they have shown me unlimited hospitality.'

Allegra listened to it all with astonishment. Her aunt had told her of their visit to the Grange but no more.

'You cannot have had as much time as you would wish to enjoy your new house,' she said. 'And you have this railway on your hands, and I suppose there will be others when this is done.'

'No,' he said decidedly. 'It will be my last. I shall be ready to advise, if my advice is sought, but no more.'

'Mamma says that everyone in Paragay is speculating upon your future wife,' she said as she poured out more coffee for him. 'Is she pretty?'

'I would not call her pretty,' he replied equably, his eyes on her face. 'Beautiful is the word I would use, I think.'

'And when are you to be married?' asked Allegra pleasantly, as if the matter was of no moment to her.

'That is a question that has not yet come up between us,' said the engineer gravely.

'You cannot mean that you have bought the Grange and furnished it for her without asking her if she will marry you?' She sounded astounded and then the thought came to her with a touch of bitterness that of course no woman could refuse him, even without the Grange at Paragay for her future home.

'The lady I have in mind,' he told her, 'is not likely to be influenced lightly by position or even by – wealth. Not that I possess wealth to compare with – say – Mr Hudson!'

She asked rather hesitantly what sort of position the

164

lady held and was told a trifle brusquely that until recently it had been a menial one in a large household. She remembered then that his mother had been a house-maid and she thought that perhaps his future wife had been a housemaid too. She changed the subject by enquiring after the gardens at the Grange, and was told of the hot-house where he planned to install hot pipes, and he admitted that the head gardener did not frighten him as much as his housekeeper, who scared him out of his wits.

They finished breakfast companionably and there was no sign of any furious pursuit from Castle Fether-stone as she stood beside him on the platform wearing her veiled hat again and waiting for the Birmingham train, due into Bending Junction at ten o'clock. Farther down the platform a groom stood holding Briony.

'When you arrive in Paragay,' her companion told her, 'the man there has instructions to take Briony to my stables, and if you care to have her stabled there indefinitely it would give me pleasure, and you easier access to her than if she went back to Lakesby.'

The train came in with a great bustle and scream of steam and having bought her ticket he found a first-class carriage occupied by one lady and her maid. He asked if she were going as far as Paragay and when she said she was he asked her to take Allegra under her protection as she was to alight there.

The lady was all graciousness. Yes, she would cer-tainly see that the young lady was aware when the train reached Paragay. Her maid was despatched to a second-class carriage a little farther down the train, because it was a mixed one, Mr Buckhurst raised his hat and went back to see that Briony and her groom were properly installed and then mounted into a first-class carriage himself *en route* for Birmingham.

It was obvious, Allegra thought, that he had no desire to make the return journey to Paragay in her company, but in the meantime he could not have chosen a better companion for her than the lady sitting opposite. As the train drew out of the station she put back her veil.

'Allegra Lakesby!' exclaimed Lady Alicia. 'I wondered if it could be you, but I was not sure because of your veil. Is this another escapade, my dear?'

'Oh, Lady Alicia,' said Allegra humbly. 'Dearest Lady Alicia. You were right and I was wrong. It is no escapade. I am going home.'

15

The door of Number 14 Well Walk was opened by Ratcliffe, their butler at the Manor, who was delighted to see her again, while Allegra was no less delighted to see him.

'I knew my mamma was to engage a manservant,' she said. 'But I did not guess that it could be you.'

'It was the work, Miss Allegra. Me not being so young these days, and all the entertaining there is at the Manor now, with Miss Rose and her young friends, and balls at night and dinner parties, the gentlemen playing cards till late. And then Mr Robert and Mrs Robert and the children coming in and out. I am too old for such work now, and when Mr Eustace suggested I should come here to my old mistress I packed up and left. I think the mistress and Miss Bell are as pleased as I am, miss, over the new arrangement.'

'I am sure they are, Ratcliffe.' Allegra walked into the little parlour unannounced and her welcome from Mrs Lakesby and her aunt was all that she could have wished.

'I hoped you would come home instead of going to Webberley,' said Laura. 'Your father was a great friend of Viscount Melton and used to go and visit there before he was married. I remember him telling me how bitterly cold it was up there in Cheshire. But of course he went in the winter and it is now summer. And what a delightful summer we have had, have we not, Bell?'

'Delightful,' echoed Bell happily. 'And all owing to our dear William.'

'William?' Allegra searched her memory in vain for a Lakesby cousin of that name.

'Mr Buckhurst, child,' said her mother, smiling. 'The dearest, kindest man on earth. You know, of course, that if it had not been for him I should not have had all that money for Masterson's? Though I still think, whatever Eustace says, that it was Mr Cruikshank who was to blame more than Barnabas. If he had not been so prejudiced against the railways Barnabas would never have had any say in the matter at all.'

Allegra led her away from Barnabas and back to Mr Buckhurst. Of what did his kindness consist?

'Why, my dear, whenever he sends his carriage for Mrs Willoughby to take her out into the country to visit her old friends, he has told her to make sure that we would not like to accompany her. And as the friends she visits are often old friends of ours too, it has been a most charming arrangement. Such beautiful carriages too, Allegra, closed for bad weather and open for fine days. We have had some delightful excursions, and it has been a most pleasant summer. I do not know when I have enjoyed a summer so much since your dear papa died.'

Allegra experienced a quite unreasonable sense of injury. Here in Paragay her mamma and her aunt had been enjoying themselves with carriage drives and visits to old friends, while she had spent the summer months being governess to little Susanna, taking her for walks, teaching her to make capital letters, and in being persecuted by her tiresome brother. She almost wished that she had gone to Webberley: then there would have been no need for Mr Buckhurst to extend his kindness to her family by looking after Briony and herself on their journey that day. Unaccountably she felt not a little neglected and ill-used by them all.

She was not made any more comfortable when a little while later her trunks arrived, having been sent to the Paragay Parcels Office without a word from Lady

Fetherstone. Her only knowledge of how her flight had been taken was in a short letter from Sarah from Webberley a week or so afterwards, scolding her for running away, and adding that her mamma had been furious and would not allow her name to be mentioned. It seemed, however, that when he was told about her sudden departure old Lord Webberley had chuckled until they thought he must have a fit, and had finally gasped out, 'So she bolted, bless the girl. She bolted.' *We are all sure*, wrote Sarah, *from the look in the wicked old man's eyes, that he had something to do with it. Do not tell me if you would rather not, Allegra, my love, but he did, didn't he?*

Allegra would not have dreamed of telling tales against Sarah's grandfather, but when she thought about the old earl and his advice that morning in the little stone temple, she knew that it had been due to him that she had escaped from the wretched Tulip Tree.

Mr Buckhurst was now fully engaged on the final plans of the Bending Junction–Worcester Railway Company, and weeks passed before he was to visit Paragay again, and in his absence Allegra had Briony removed to the livery stables next to the Coach and Horses, although her mamma and her aunt said they did not think dear William would like it. Allegra was determined not to be in the man's debt herself, whatever her mamma and aunt might say, although she found that her rides were often inclined to take her past the Grange.

When she looked at the long, pretty house, with its creepers over the porch and the windows open, with new curtains blowing in the breeze, and when she saw the well-kept drive and the dear little park and the great cedar tree, she envied the fortunate woman who was to live there with William Buckhurst, and she wondered rather sadly if she realized the treasure she was to find there besides the house and its fine position and its owner's money.

Because, as she listened to his praises from all quarters in the little town until she declared to the Rector's daughters that she was getting tired of the sound of his name, she began to realize more and more that it was the man himself who counted in Paragay, and not what he had. Lady Maria Huckley had told her stories of Hudson the Railway King and his vulgar wife, and how everyone fawned on them because of the vast fortune he had made from speculation in rail shares, but William Buckhurst was not like that and the residents of Paragay knew it. His money and house might have attracted them in the first place, but when those things were assimilated it was the man himself that remained for them to like and to respect, as Allegra had liked and respected him on that journey to Bending Junction, when her cousin Robert handed her over to him like a bale of goods to be delivered to the parcels office there.

She wondered if part of the reason why she had disliked Oliver so much was because she had carried the picture of this man with her to Castle Fetherstone. He was the sort of man to treat all women alike, with courtesy and gentleness, whether they were rich or poor, old or young. She hoped that his future wife, coming from 'a menial' position in a great household, would not let herself be frightened by his dragon of a housekeeper, but she was very much afraid that she would.

．　　．　　．　　．　　．

If Allegra had hoped that she would hear no more from Oliver she soon found herself to be mistaken. On his arrival at Webberley, having heard the full story of her iniquity from his mamma, his lordship listened to what she had to say and then started off for Lakesby Manor.

The result of his visit there was that one morning Eustace called on his cousin's widow in Well Walk and asked if he might speak to Allegra.

She came, as she done on that previous occasion, to the dining-parlour and found him in much the same grave mood as he had been then.

'Allegra,' he said at once. 'I have Lord Fetherstone with me, and he wishes to speak to you. I expect you know what it is about.'

'Oh dear!' She was dismayed. 'He is not being tiresome again?'

'If by being tiresome you mean that he has made a formal proposal for your hand, through me as head of your family, then, my dear, he has been tiresome.' He came to her and put his hand kindly on her shoulder. 'Allegra, my dear, he tells me that he has been in love with you ever since he first saw you, and that he wants to marry you as soon as you feel you can do so. You will not get a better match in the whole of England. He is a most excellent young man.'

'But I do not want to marry him,' she said. 'I am very sorry, Cousin Eustace, but if I had wished to do so I would have gone to Webberley with his family.'

'But do you dislike him then?' Eustace could not understand her.

'I do not dislike him,' she said, tears in her eyes. 'Indeed, sir, I do not. But I do not like him sufficiently to marry him.'

'Well, he is not likely to take a refusal from me,' said her cousin. 'I told him that for my part he had my full permission to pay his addresses to you. You must make your refusal of them yourself. He is out there in my carriage and I will send him in.'

'No – Cousin Eustace, please!' She tried to stop him but in vain.

'I will be very displeased if you do not see Lord Fetherstone yourself, Allegra,' he said. 'I can only think that your running away from Fetherstone – yes, you may well blush, for I have heard all about it – was simply another of your ridiculous escapades, and that you will now think more seriously about your future.'

In a few minutes he was gone and Oliver was with her.

'Allegra,' he said, taking her hands, 'all I ask from you is a promise that I may hope. It is not too much to ask for, is it?'

'But I cannot give it to you,' she said sadly. 'I am sorry, Oliver, but how can I raise your hopes if they cannot be fulfilled? I cannot marry you.'

He dropped her hands. 'You dislike me so much?'

She shook her head in silence, afraid of bursting into tears. How could she explain that she could not make one of the Tulip Tree, even if she loved him? She would be mistress of Castle Fetherstone in name only: the Dowager Lady Fetherstone would always be in command. If she ordered a carriage she would want to know why, if she planned a dinner party her ladyship would have to be consulted, to approve or disapprove of the guests she wished to invite. Oliver's wife would only be a figurehead in his house, his mamma would still be its real mistress, and that Allegra knew she could not and would not endure. Better by far to be single all her life here in little Paragay than held in Castle Fetherstone where the fleshpots would be bitter indeed and the dungeons very deep.

Oliver guessed something of what was going on in her mind.

'It is Mamma, is it not?' he said. 'You are afraid of being dragooned by her for the rest of your life. It is my family that is the root of the trouble, not only me.'

He was right of course, yet how could she tell him

so? She was not an earl's daughter, she was the daughter of a country gentleman, accustomed to having servants about her, but servants she had known all her life. There had never been more than a couple of footmen at Lakesby, not six in red plush, powdered hair and silk stockings, just to stand about in a great hall. Castle Fetherstone and the Tulip Tree would swallow her up between them and she would never be herself again. She had longed for large rooms, but not the impersonal rooms of Castle Fetherstone, where pictures had histories, and where statues stood about in cold white marble along great corridors. She wanted a house that was warm and her own, not a vast establishment where she could never be more than a passing tenant.

'I do not think you know how determined your mother can be,' she told him. 'The Bending–Worcester Railway will never run through Fetherstone land, but through the Spender property instead. Did you not wonder why Sir Gilbert Buttrell was at your coming-of-age? Your mamma was collecting her forces, so that she could have his promise to throw the Bill out in committee.' She broke off. 'But I ought not to be saying this. It is nothing to do with me.'

'Where did you get your information from?' he demanded. 'Who told you?'

'Your grandfather, on the day of your coming-of-age.'

'And he would know what he was saying,' he muttered. 'So that was why the member for Sprackley was at Fetherstone that day. I thought he was there as my guest, not to rob me. And I begin to comprehend why I have had no word from the railway, with papers for my signature. No doubt they knew what was in the wind.' He walked to the window and stood there, staring at the windows of the house opposite without seeing them. Then he turned.

'I suppose there is somebody else,' he said. 'You are in love with another man?'

'No of course not.' He thought her denial a shade too quick.

'I thought it might be Buckhurst,' he said. 'Sarah said you were talking to him that day, and your cousin said he had been kind to your mother.'

'Mr Buckhurst is a very kind man,' she said. 'But he is nothing to do with me. He came to see you that day at Fetherstone, but I daresay he had seen Sir Gilbert Buttrell and heard something that made him think the planning of his railroad through your land would be a waste of time. Oh, it is all guesswork of course, and if you were to tax your mamma with having had any part in it you would come off worst in the encounter.'

'You need say no more. I shall make up my own mind what I shall say to my mother, but there is one thing clear in my mind. From now on I shall be master in my own house.' He took her hand and held it for a moment in a warm grasp. 'Try not to think of us too badly,' he said, 'and if you can, keep a little kindness in your heart for me.'

He did not know how near he came to winning her then. 'I shall always think of you with kindness,' she told him. 'I only wish my feeling for you could be more.'

After he had gone she had to endure her mother's disappointment and her aunt's gentle reproaches. Her cousin Eustace had told them that Lord Fetherstone was very much in love with her. Could she not bring herself to return his devotion?

'I had only set eyes on your papa twice before my father told me I was to marry him,' said Laura plaintively. 'And I could not have had a better or more loving husband.'

Allegra remembered sadly that Mr Buckhurst had accused her of being a rebel. 'I want to marry a man I

can love with my whole heart,' she said. 'I cannot marry
Lord Fetherstone – or his family – or that horrid Tulip
Tree!' And she ran up to her room to cry her heart out,
weeping for she did not know what, but it might have
been for a man who had looked after her on her first
escapade and again on her last. A man who would
inspire respect as well as love, whose heart was already
given to a horrid little housemaid who would not appreciate him a little bit.

The news of her refusal of Oliver was soon circulating
among the young Lakesbys' friends, and she found it
hard to maintain her composure in the face of their
merciless teasing.

Why did she refuse Lord Fetherstone? they wanted
to know. Was he not good-looking enough for her?
Rose asked, while Elaine told her frankly that she was
the biggest goose she had ever known.

'We knew you to be a madcap,' Robert added.
'But we did not think you to be capable of such utter
folly. Oliver Fetherstone is an excellent fellow, and
surely his houses and estates are fine enough for you?'

Only a few months ago she might have agreed with
her cousins. When she had started out for Fetherstone
on the first day of March her thoughts had dwelt on its
young owner very pleasantly indeed. If her opinion of
him had changed with experience, so now that she was
home again, had her attitude towards her old Lakesby
home.

The rooms might be smaller than those at Fetherstone and more homely, but it was somebody else's
home now and not hers, and she did not care about it
any more. She discovered too that her old friends had
shifted their allegiance to Rose and to Robert and
Elaine, and that although she was included in their
parties it was with some curiosity and open amusement
at her latest escapade.

None of them believed that she could have been serious in her rejection of Lord Fetherstonè and when he did not pursue his wish to marry her they pitied her for her disappointment. She should have made sure of him, they told her, while she had the chance.

All this Allegra found it extremely hard to bear, and she began to make excuses for not accompanying her mamma and aunt to Lakesby. When she went riding she could at least avoid her cousins and their friends now that Briony was housed in Paragay, although Laura protested that she should not go without a groom to accompany her.

'My poor Allegra,' Laura said to Bell one afternoon when her daughter had gone off on one of her solitary rides. 'She was upset enough at leaving Lakesby, but now that she has got over it and is back in Paragay she does not seem to be any happier, although all her old friends seem prepared to make much of her these days.'

'I think they tease her somewhat,' said Bell cheerfully. 'And Allegra always had a temper, from a little girl.'

'So she had,' agreed Mrs Henry Lakesby fondly. 'I do hope she will not take another post as a governess!'

'She told me when she came home it was a situation she would never undertake again.' Bell's common sense was comforting. 'She will soon be our own Allegra again, you see if she will not. Why, only last evening the Major had her laughing over a game of whist. Very gallant is the Major. He asked her if she had seen Mr Buckhurst lately, and chuckled when she blushed. Poor Allegra. The whole world seems bent on teasing her.'

In the meantime her rides took her past the Grange on her way to the open country beyond, returning to the livery stables by way of the common above Well Walk.

The first of October was fine and sunny, and Briony was as happy to be out in the sunshine as she was herself. Their road took them past the Grange as usual, where she saw windows open and the front of the house bathed in mellow sunshine, turning the leaves of the creeper over the porch to scarlet and gold.

She wondered when Mr Buckhurst would be returning, and if his bride would come with him, and rode on thinking of him, and the deep blue eyes that had seemed to see into her heart. She remembered his care for her on the two journeys, his blunt directness that was so different and so much more attractive than the schoolboy vapourings of Oliver, and of his care for Briony.

On the wrong side of the door, he had said. But he could never be on the wrong side of any door. It was the man that mattered, not his family, and he did not have to live in a mansion to prove it.

She was returning down the lane from the turnpike to the common when she heard horse's hoofs behind her and Bucephalus was reined in beside her.

'Miss Allegra!' William Buckhurst was annoyed. 'I told you to keep Briony at the Grange, and I find that for the past month or so she has been accommodated at the livery stables in Paragay, and that you have been out riding unaccompanied. If she had been in my stables one of my grooms would have gone with you. You might have had an accident and been thrown on one of your solitary rides.'

'Briony is quiet and good-tempered. She is not likely to shy at anything or to throw me.' She reined in the little mare however and Briony joined Bucephalus in cropping the grass under the trees while Allegra went on to say that she did not mean to show ingratitude, but that his kindness to her family had been so great already that she had felt she could not trespass on his good nature as well.

'No,' he said shortly. 'I suppose you would not.' He muttered something about independence and that a woman could have too much of it, and then suddenly his ill-humour vanished and he turned to her with his old understanding smile. The lane was lined with trees, and the oaks there were beginning to turn, but the branches were thick with leaves and met overhead making a tunnel like the one that was to be made under Bending High Street. The fact that he was beside her and that she could hear his voice again was all that mattered, and she did not care if that voice held nothing but reproof.

He continued in a gentler tone, 'I have heard that his lordship came to Well Walk to see you and that you sent him to the right about. Your cousin Eustace was very angry when he told me about it, and when I suggested that your refusal might be due to maidenly confusion or uncertainty he told me not to be a fool. "Allegra has never been maidenly or confused in her life," he said. "She has always known very well what she is doing." Is that true, Miss Allegra?'

'Not quite.' Her eyes met his honestly because with him she had to speak the truth. 'I did not know what I was doing when I left Paragay for Fetherstone, but I knew very well what I was doing when I left Fetherstone and when I refused to marry its owner.' She sighed with a touch of impatience. 'I wish people would understand that, instead of giving me a character for weakness and vacillation.'

He seemed content to sit there beside her while Bucephalus and Briony cropped the grass under the trees.

'I have planned my railway,' he said, 'and the Bill will be through Parliament this month – there is no doubt about that. By November the contractor and his gangs will have started their labours and my work, except for a weekly visit or so to supervise it, will be concluded.' He paused and went on quietly, 'I have often taken risks in what I have had to do and say, but never quite as great a risk as I am about to take now – it includes the possible loss of my friendship with your mamma and your aunt and the respect of their friends. I must also risk your cousin Eustace's anger and the mockery of those who are not so fond of me, fancying me to be too big for my boots. But these are things that must be risked and there is no help for it. Will you marry me, Allegra, child? Or will I always be on the wrong side of the door?'

She had put back the veil from her face while they were talking and as she turned to face him he saw her lips tremble and the dark eyes fill, and perhaps because the moment was so grave for them both she tried to laugh.

'You know how much money and position count with me,' she said. 'How can I refuse wealth and the Grange?'

His left hand gripped hers. 'Stop teasing,' he told her sternly, 'and answer my question. It's myself I'm offering you, and I know I'm not much of a bargain.'

'But one does not look for bargains when one marries, but for quality.' Her smile trembled out at him. 'How could you be Mamma's and Aunt Bell's "dearest William" all this time and not mine as well?'

'So it is to be yes?' he said. He took the glove off the hand in his and raised it to his lips, and as they rode on together he told her with quiet sincerity that he had fallen in love with her when he saw her on Paragay platform on the first of March, with her lovely hair shining from under her straw bonnet. 'I am glad you chose to wear that brown dress, however much your cousin abused it,' he said. 'If you had been dressed as grandly as you were at the coming-of-age at Fetherstone I do not suppose I would have given you a second thought. But in that dress you were my equal. I felt I could talk to you, and think of you as I would.'

As they turned their horses' heads towards the common she asked him why he had told her at breakfast at the stationmaster's house that the woman he hoped to marry was in a menial position.

'I said I believe that she *had* been in a menial position,' he corrected her. 'There perhaps I was wrong, but in a place the size of Castle Fetherstone I imagine governessing might be classed as a menial occupation.'

'It was indeed!' She shivered. 'Oh how I came to hate that great house!'

'Do you think you will like the Grange better?'

'I shall love it.' Had she not loved it more and more every time she had passed it on Briony?

'I must warn you that my housekeeper is a dragon.'

'I shall manage her, my dearest,' said Allegra with a confidence that turned out not to be misplaced.

16

About the same time that Allegra's engagement to Mr Buckhurst became public property, Lady Fetherstone and her family returned to Castle Fetherstone, where Mrs Glynn met them with a long face. To her ladyship's enquiry as to whether his lordship was in London, as he was not there to welcome them, she replied that he was out riding and she expected him back shortly.

'The truth is, m'lady,' she said, 'his lordship has been acting very strange of late.'

'Strange? What can you mean?' Lady Fetherstone went into the room that had always been her favourite sitting-room and stopped short. Her French furniture and pretty furnishings had gone, with her personal possessions, and in their place were heavy chairs and tables from Oliver's private sitting-room, and a desk that had belonged to his father. The housekeeper followed her into the room almost in tears.

'It was after his lordship came back from Paragay, m'lady,' she said. 'The first thing he did was to go into the picture gallery and take down that picture of the tulip tree and smash it over his knee. Then he ordered it to be burnt.'

'But – ' Grizelda stared at her housekeeper in dismay. 'Did he give any reason for doing it?'

'No, m'lady. He was in such a black rage that I dursn't question him. Then he went off to London and when he came back he was in a blacker rage still, and he had this room changed, and that was not the only change he made neither. I had never seen him like that before. It worried me so much that I couldn't sleep a wink last night, what with knowing your ladyship would be home today, and the storm we had in the night – thunder and lightning till daybreak. I felt sure the house must be struck.' There was the sound of heavy footsteps crossing the great hall and Oliver's voice giving direction to one of the servants there, and she said with relief, 'Here is his lordship now, m'lady.' And fled.

Her ladyship waited Oliver's entrance with puzzlement and a little apprehension, wondering if his disappointment over Allegra had turned his brain.

He came in with scarcely a smile, gave his cheek for her to kiss, greeted his sisters perfunctorily, and shook hands with his brothers. Then he glanced round the room in which they were standing and said, 'I see that Mrs Glynn has shown you some of my alterations here, Mamma. The thing is, of course, that I have moved into my father's rooms – as they are now mine – and I knew you would not object if I had your apartments situated in the west wing, knowing how much you admire the view towards the Copley hills. You will be glad to know that there will be no railway there to spoil that view, although you may experience some slight inconvenience from a small private gasometer that I intend to have installed in the west shrubberies. If you should find it too objectionable the Dower House is empty and at your disposal.' Before she could open her mouth he continued in the same level voice, with no trace of feeling in it, 'Sir Giles Spender is delighted that the railway is to go through his property – it has, I understand, just saved him from bankruptcy. I was not so fortunate, and as I shall not have the money I had intended to use for the improvements I promised my tenants here and in Yorkshire, I have had to look for economies elsewhere. You will be pleased to hear I am sure that I have let my house in Eaton Square to your good friend, Sir Gilbert Buttrell. He has been searching for a suitable house in

London while the House is sitting, and his wife is delighted with it.'

'You have dared to let the Eaton Square house without my permission?' Grizelda was furious, and then she saw him smile, and something in that smile reminded her of her old father when he thought he had done something particularly clever.

'I think you have forgotten, Mamma,' said Oliver smoothly, 'that I do not need to ask anyone's permission for what I do with my own property.' He turned as the door was thrown open and Susanna ran into the room.

'Oliver!' she cried. 'Do you know what has happened? Nurse Capper has just told me that in the storm last night the tulip tree was struck by lightning and it has been split right down the middle and she reckons it is stone dead!'

'And a good thing too,' said Oliver, and sent for Mrs Glynn to show his mamma her rooms in the west wing.

Grizelda examined them in silence. It occurred to her then for the first time that what she had been warned would happen had come to pass, and that her own part in it might have been a disaster. Her son Oliver had grown up, and his manner implied that as head of the family he expected to command its attention and respect.

That evening she wrote to Mr Armitage, telling him of Oliver's extraordinary behaviour and demanding his immediate presence at Fetherstone. His reply was prompt and brief.

My dear Grizel, he wrote, *I am extremely glad to hear that Oliver is showing such an interest in his new position as head of the family. I fear that I shall be unable to visit Fetherstone for some time to come as I am leaving tonight for a long sojourn in the Hebrides. Your devoted J.A.*

It was left to the eldest Miss Dalrymple to say the last word about Allegra's marriage, after it had taken place that Christmas.

'All that talk about her refusing Lord Fetherstone,' she said with a toss of her head. 'I knew there was not a word of truth in it. It was Buckhurst she was after, encouraged no doubt by Mrs Lakesby and Miss Bell.'

'I understand they are spending their wedding trip in Paris,' said the younger Miss Dalrymple wistfully. 'When they return, will you call on them, Ellen?'

Miss Dalrymple considered the matter judicially. Then she pronounced, 'As these railway persons are considered by some to be our new gentry, I suppose I must call.' Not for the world would she admit to a vulgar curiosity as to what the Grange was like now that this particular railway person was its master.

She remembered how a little while ago she had complained to the Major that the railway barons were knocking at their gates, and it would not be long before they had their feet inside their doors. Whereupon the foolish old man had replied with a knowing look, 'Then do you not think, Miss Dalrymple, the civil thing would be to open our doors and ask them to step inside?'

'I shall wait until they are home and have come to church,' she said tolerantly. 'And then we will have a carriage from the livery stables and call upon Mr and Mrs Buckhurst.'

It would be interesting to see for herself if what Mrs Henry Lakesby had said was true: that the colouring of every room in the Grange had been carefully selected by William Buckhurst as a background for his wife's beautiful hair.

JANETTE SEYMOUR

PURITY'S SHAME

The fervour that blazed across the pages of PURITY'S PASSION and PURITY'S ECSTASY now sweeps Purity to the consummate moment of her star-crossed destiny. From a French chateau to a mansion on the Popomac, through the crime-ridden slums and reeking jails of regency London to the splendours of a royal coronation, from the arms of one lustful deceiver to the next, she follows her dreams of undying love – ever seeking her beloved Mark Landless, who desires her above all else in the world!

CORONET BOOKS

ANNA GILBERT

THE LEAVETAKING

Life at Emberside Grange was quiet but pleasant for
Isobel, her widowed father and her older half-cousin
Lydia whom she adored. Pleasant, that is, until the
day portrait artist Simeon Graw, with his black cloak
and unkempt beard, walks into their lives. Suddenly
Lydia vanishes. In the dark months that follow, Isobel
engages in a desperate and dangerous search for her
beloved cousin. And nothing is so cruel as the truth
that awaits her on her return to Emberside.

CORONET BOOKS

MALCOLM MACDONALD

ABIGAIL

Born to riches and a high place in Victorian society, bred to innocence and idleness, Abigail is the gifted and headstrong daughter of the great railway Stevensons.

Bent on independence and determined never to marry, Abigail leaves behind her first and deepest love and her brilliant professional career in London, setting out on a wild and unconventional search for self-realisation. As she plunges into the luxurious heights and brutal depths of Victorian Europe, she learns that she knew nothing of the extraordinary power of love – and the tyranny of desire.

'Malcolm Macdonald is the heir to the Delderfield kingdom'

Philadelphia Inquirer

CORONET BOOKS

ROSELEEN MILNE

THE MAJOR'S LADY

When sixteen-year-old Dorinda Fane and her dashing
Army husband set sail for French-held Portugal in the
year 1808, her dreams of happiness were already
shattered. But the disillusionment of her wedding
night in no way prepared her for the personal
devastation of that winter campaign.

As the blood-soaked and disease-ridden columns
stagger rebelliously through the Iberian mountains
with Napoleon's cavalry at their heels, Dindie's
marriage to Kit must reach its own shaming
climax . . .

'A brilliant portrait of the winter campaign in Portugal
against Napoleon, and deep understanding of a young
English girl's frustrated love'.

Evening News

CORONET BOOKS

ALSO AVAILABLE IN CORONET BOOKS

ROSELEEN MILNE

☐ 26672 4   The Major's Lady   £1.40

MALCOLM MACDONALD

☐ 23330 8   The Rich Are With You Always   £1.75
☐ 20010 3   World From Rough Stones   £1.75
☐ 24170 5   Sons of Fortune   £1.50
☐ 26216 8   Abigail   £1.95

ANNA GILBERT

☐ 26683 X   The Leavetaking   £1.10

JANETTE SEYMOUR

☐ 22942 X   Purity's Passion   £1.25
☐ 23774 O   Purity's Shame   £1.50

All these books are available at your local bookshop or newagent, or can be ordered direct from the publisher. Just tick the titles you want and fill in the form below.

Prices and availability subject to change without notice.

CORONET BOOKS, P.O. Box 11, Falmouth, Cornwall.

Please send cheque or postal order, and allow the following for postage and packing:

U.K. – 40p for one book plus 18p for the second book, and 13p for each additional book ordered up to a £1.49 maximum.

B.F.P.O. and EIRE – 40p for the first book, plus 18p for the second book, and 13p per copy for the next 7 books, 7p per book thereafter.

OTHER OVERSEAS CUSTOMERS – 60p for the first book, plus 18p per copy for each additional book.

Name...

Address..

....